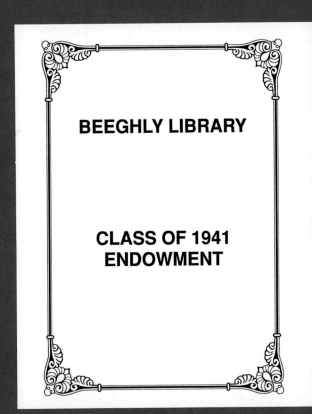

The Day *of the* Pelican

The Day *of the* Pelican

KATHERINE PATERSON

CLARION BOOKS
Houghton Mifflin Harcourt
Boston • New York
2009

Clarion Books
215 Park Avenue South, New York, New York 10003
Copyright © 2009 by Minna Murra, Inc.

The text was set in 12-point Goudy.

Clarion Books is an imprint of Houghton Mifflin Harcourt Publishing Company.

www.hmhbooks.com

Printed in the United States of America

Library of Congress Cataloging-in-Publication Data

Paterson, Katherine.
The day of the pelican / by Katherine Paterson.
p. cm.
"Houghton Mifflin Harcourt."
Summary: In 1998 when the Kosovo hostilities escalate, the life of thirteen-year-old Meli, an
ethnic Albanian, changes forever after her brother escapes his Serbian captors and the entire
family flees from one refugee camp to another until they are able to immigrate to America.
ISBN 978-0-547-18188-2
[1. Refugees—Fiction. 2. Refugee camps—Fiction. 3. Muslims—Fiction. 4. Albanians—
Kosovo—Fiction. 5. Kosovo War, 1998–1999—Fiction. 6. Kosovo (Republic)—History—
1980–2008—Fiction. 7. United States—History—20th century—Fiction.] I. Title.

PZ7.P273Day 2009
[Fic]—dc22
2009014998

MP 10 9 8 7 6 5 4 3 2 1

This book is for
Muhamet, Saveta, Elez, Yllka, Almedina, and Aridon Haxhiu,
whose family story planted the seed,
and for
Mark Orfila,
without whose help it could not have come to fruition.

"I am like a pelican of the wilderness,
I am like an owl out of the desert.
I watch and am as a sparrow alone upon the housetop."
—Psalm 102:6–7 King James Version

"The Family is the Country of the heart."
—Giuseppe Mazzini, *The Duties of Man*

CONTENTS

ONE

The Lleshis of Kosovo

TERRIBLE THINGS SHOULD NEVER HAPPEN IN SPRINGTIME, and it was almost spring. March had arrived on the Plain of Dukagjin, and even though most days were still bitter with the raw dampness of late winter, they were getting longer. Today had been one of those rare, bright days promising that spring would eventually come. The afternoon sun fell warm on Meli's hands as she took in the wash Mama had hung out this morning. In the light breeze the multicolored plastic clothespins danced like little people atop the line. She should remember that thought—put it into a poem, or at least tell Zana at school the next day. They shared silly thoughts, she and Zana. That's why they were best friends—that and the fact that both their fathers had come from farm villages and so weren't proper "citizens" in the eyes of their classmates whose families had long lived in town. They weren't looked down on like Gypsies or hated like Serbs, but still, there was a difference, and she and Zana knew it and shared it.

Meli dropped Baba's best shirt into the basket at her feet and took a deep breath. Was there a smell of spring in the air? She longed for spring, when the two cherry trees in the back corner of the garden would bloom and the storks would return from their winter vacation in Africa. She tried to imagine the great birds flying over that immense continent, across Saudi Arabia and Turkey. Or did they choose a more daring flight over the

Mediterranean Sea to come home to Kosovo? She'd have to ask Mr. Uka. Their teacher liked to be asked unusual questions. It gave him a chance to show off a bit, tell them about his trip years ago to the shore of the Adriatic Sea.

Meli had never seen any sea. She had never been anywhere, really. But she had seen pictures on television of oceans larger than the Mediterranean. Mr. Uka had said that there were birds that crossed those oceans in their migrations—tiny birds, far smaller than the white storks. How brave that seemed. The thought of traveling as far as Prishtina made her stomach flutter.

Meli finished taking in the first line of clothes and started on the second. Beyond the bounds of the town she could see green patches of winter wheat and, in the distant west, the snow-capped Albanian Alps—the "Cursed Mountains," people called them, but no one seemed to know quite why. To the south was the Sharr range, where, she had been told, wild horses ran free. She had seen them only in her imagination, but that didn't make them less real, their manes streaming in the wind as they raced about joyfully, unseen, unheard, unthreatened by the petty hatreds of humankind.

It would be a long time before spring came to those heights, but the snow was already beginning to melt on the hillsides. The gold cross and red-tiled roof of an old Serbian Christian church stood out starkly against the grays and browns of late winter. *Why do the Serbs hate us so?* Though, to be honest, most Albanians hated the Serbs just as fiercely. Some of the girls at school could, and would, recite terrible poems against the Serbs. She could never understand hate like that. Baba had always taught them to respect, not to hate. But he was not like other people. Even now, just a few feet away, her two little brothers were playing war. Was that fun? It must be. They played it every day, although they knew Baba disapproved. She tried to think of spring and blossoms and the return of birdsong to the garden.

Adil's yell broke her reverie. "Meli! Tell Isuf I'm the KLA man!"

"No," Isuf said with the practiced authority of the older brother. "You're a Serb. *I'm* the KLA soldier."

"Meli!" Adil begged. "Isuf always makes me be a Serb policeman. Tell him to let me be the KLA man. It's my turn."

Meli sighed, keeping her eyes on Vlora's frilly new dress as she took it off the line. She wouldn't want to drop it; the ground was still muddy. "Stop fighting, boys. If you can't take turns, find some other game to play."

It was Mehmet's fault. Their older brother was convinced that the Kosovo Liberation Army would soon save the Albanians. No matter what Baba said, Mehmet worshiped the KLA. Baba said they were more legend than fact, but Mehmet was convinced they were simply biding their time, waiting for a chance to free Kosovo from Serbian domination. Even Mr. Uka, pointing to the picture on their classroom wall of Skanderbeg, the Kosovars' fifteenth-century hero, predicted that out of the KLA would arise a new Skanderbeg who would liberate Kosovo.

She must have heard the familiar rattle and roar without realizing it: Uncle Fadil's ancient Lada Niva. Baba, as elder brother of the Lleshi family, had tried to convince him to sell it and buy a new tractor, but Uncle Fadil had refused. The Lada suited him. He had taken out the back seat so he could load the car for market. Ten years of carrying vegetables, chickens, and the occasional goat had not dealt kindly with the old Russian-made vehicle. It was something of a family joke. "Well," Mehmet would say, "you can always tell when Uncle Fadil is arriving— if not by the noise, then certainly by the smell." But the truth was, Meli was distracted, and she wasn't aware that the car had driven up until the brakes squawked and it pulled to a stop on the street in front of the store.

She dodged under the clothesline and ran around the edge of the building to see. Yes, it was Uncle Fadil's car, but what was it doing here in the late afternoon? He should be home milking his cow and goats at this time of day.

"Isuf, Adil, run into the store and tell Baba that Uncle Fadil is here," Meli said.

"I don't want to go in. It's my turn to be the KLA man."

Just then the driver's door opened. It took Uncle Fadil three tries to get it slammed shut again. Meanwhile, the passenger door opened, and his wife stepped out onto the curb. Why had Auntie Burbuqe come and left Granny alone on the farm? She never did that.

"Come on, Adil, let's get Baba." Isuf's eyes were wide with fear. Even at eight he was old enough to realize that something was dreadfully wrong if both his aunt and uncle arrived unannounced.

A chill went through Meli. She called out to her uncle, "Is Granny all right?"

Uncle Fadil looked up, startled. "Granny? Yes, yes, of course."

So it was something else. "I'll—I'll tell Mama you're here," Meli said, and raced around the building and up the outside stairs to the apartment above the store before slipping off her shoes at the door.

Before long, the whole family was assembled in the parlor: Uncle Fadil and Auntie Burbuqe took the two upholstered chairs, while Baba, Mama with Vlora on her lap, and Mehmet sat on the couch. Adil and Isuf propped themselves against their father's knees. There was no place for Meli to sit except for the tiny stool in front of the television set, so she chose instead to lean against the frame of the kitchen door. Everyone was still, waiting. Even her long-dead grandfather and grandmother seemed to be staring out of their black-and-white photograph atop the television set, watching Uncle Fadil as he nervously rubbed his large black mustache.

At last he put his hand in his lap and cleared his throat. He half nodded toward the two little boys and Vlora, as though signaling to his brother, and jerked his head toward Meli.

Mama looked puzzled; then she caught Baba's eye and said, "Meli, take the little ones into the kitchen. If there's no mineral water in the cabinet, send one of the boys down to get some. Your aunt and uncle must be thirsty after their trip." She paused, looked at both men, and then added, "Oh, and while you're out there, make some coffee. We'd all enjoy a cup, I think."

Uncle Fadil nodded, obviously relieved that he had been understood.

Baba gave the little boys a gentle shove, and Mama put Vlora down from her lap. Meli took Vlora's hand and started for the kitchen, but not before she saw the smug expression on her older brother's face. Mehmet was only thirteen, less than a year and a half older than she was. Why could he stay for the grown-ups' talk and not she?

"Come on, Isuf, Adil," she said, and pulled a reluctant Vlora behind her.

"I want to stay," said Isuf. "I want to know—"

"Come on," Meli said gruffly.

"And shut the door after you," Mama called out.

Meli left the door open a tiny crack. She couldn't help it. She had to find out what was going on. There was a bottle of mineral water in the cabinet, but even before she poured out two glasses, Mehmet got up and pulled the door completely closed.

Why was Mehmet a grownup all of a sudden? It wasn't fair. She was nearly as tall as he was and every bit as responsible. But then, her mother *had* asked her to make coffee—a job Mama usually reserved for herself.

The boys were huddled against the kitchen door. "Come away from the door, Isuf, Adil," she said as she ground the beans to a fine powder. "You mustn't eavesdrop."

"Why not?" Adil asked. Isuf ignored her and kept his ear pasted to the wood.

"It's grown-up business." She put the coffee and sugar into water and started the flame under the pot. "Isuf! You heard me. Come away from that door."

But Isuf kept his ear to the door, wanting desperately to hear the muffled conversation from the parlor. Meli tried not to worry—to concentrate on her task. She stretched on tiptoe to get four coffee cups off the top shelf. Mehmet might be there, pretending to be an adult, but she certainly wasn't going to serve him a cup of the best coffee Baba sold in the shop.

"Isuf," she said again, "I told you to come away from the door."

Isuf did turn toward her, but his face was ashen, his eyes full of terror. "Meli," he whispered. "Something terrible's happened. Somebody's dead."

"Who's dead?"

"Somebody named Adem. They killed him. Uncle Fadil said so. They killed him and all his family. Even the children."

Before Meli could think who this Adem person might be, Isuf pushed the door open, and both boys ran into the parlor and flung themselves against their father. Vlora was right behind; even at four she knew to be frightened. She ran for the safety of

6

her mother's lap and buried her face in Mama's apron. Mama picked her up and held her close. The other adults sat in stunned silence. Baba began to rub the little boys' backs with his big hands.

"Seventy people." It was Mehmet who broke the silence. "Adem Jashari and his family. Those Serb butchers just went in and slaughtered them all."

Uncle Fadil's head was down, and Meli could hardly hear him. "It is said that one child escaped—one of the little girls."

"They said he was part of the KLA—that he was threatening violence," said Mehmet. "How dare they accuse *us* of violence?"

"Meli," Mama said softly, "the mineral water? And it smells as though the coffee is ready."

Meli put the coffee cups on the tray with the glasses. Her hands shook as she poured out the strong, sweet liquid. *They aren't just killing a few men here and there. They're slaughtering whole families. What does it mean?* She tried to steady herself, but the cups rattled in their saucers as she brought the tray in and passed the mineral water and coffee to her aunt and uncle and the coffee to her parents. "Fix a cup for Mehmet," Mama said as she took her cup, "and one for yourself, too. You will have to be grown-ups now."

"Me, too," said Isuf. "I'm almost nine."

"You may have a sip of mine," Baba said. "And you, too, Adil."

"Does it have lots of sugar?"

"Yes, of course," Baba said, rubbing Adil's hair. "Meli made it just right."

Meli poured coffee for Mehmet and herself in the everyday cups and then sat down on the low stool in front of the TV set.

7

They sat in silence for a long time. Even the youngest were quiet. What would her grandparents think of this, she wondered. But they just stared out grimly from their silver frame, saying nothing.

Uncle Fadil took a noisy slurp, smoothed his mustache, and cleared his throat. "We came," he said, "we came because we want you to come home. No place is safe, but if things go—go badly, at least we will have each other."

But the house in the country isn't home. This apartment is my home. How can I leave here? Leave school and Zana? Meli couldn't bear the thought. Besides, she reasoned, if no place was safe, why not stay right where they were? *It's true that the Serb family next door no longer shops in Baba's store, and they never speak if you see them on the street. But they have been our neighbors for my whole life. Why, just four years ago, when Vlora was born, Mrs. Jokic brought over a huge cake. Surely they would never harm us. The police are annoying, but we know better than to provoke them, and they've never seriously threatened us.* Still, this Adem Jashari person and all of his large extended family were dead. *What does that mean for us? For any Albanian in Kosovo? But to leave our home . . . ?*

Everyone was looking at Baba. It was he who must decide. He took a long sip of his coffee and gave a taste to each of the little boys before he looked directly at his younger brother and answered. "Thank you, brother. You are always kind, but how can I leave my apartment and my store? My children have never known another home, and every Albanian in the neighborhood depends on me, on our store, for food. What would we do in the country? I don't even know what kind of school there is in the village." He shook his head. "On the farm we would only be a burden. Here we are among friends. Here we are needed."

"I am not being kind," Uncle Fadil said, his voice rising. "The farm is your home, brother. It is your *home* I'm talking about. It belongs to you as much as to me. You know that!"

Auntie Burbuqe half rose to her feet. "Come on! I swear to God. Are we family or not?"

Meli was startled. She'd never seen Auntie so agitated.

"You are right, Burbuqe," said Baba. "We are family, and family is more important than anything. But"—he gave a little laugh—"I grew up in that house. I know how small it is. And look at us. After those long years of waiting, Sevdie and I now find ourselves blessed with all these children. Besides, you must think of your own Nexima. With Hamza's people dead, they have no family home to go to except ours. Suppose they decide to come back from Prishtina. They have three children. That little house would burst like an overripe pumpkin."

Uncle Fadil shook his head. For a moment Meli thought he might argue, but he just stood up. "We must get back. Mother is alone. And the milking . . ." He looked about for a place to set down his empty cup and saucer, so Meli quickly fetched the tray for him. "If you change your mind, my brother, there is always room for you."

"Yes," said Auntie Burbuqe. "Please know we want you with us. All of you."

As soon as the car pulled away from in front of the store, Meli ran down to the garden to finish bringing in the clean wash. Maybe if she did something ordinary, the day would untwist itself and life would seem normal again.

❀ ❀ ❀

The cherry trees put out their pale pink blossoms against the brilliant blue of the spring sky. House martins built a new nest under the eaves. The storks made their long journey home. School went on much as usual, though everyone seemed to have a touch of spring fever. Meli was sure her father had been right to stay. Oh, in town there had been some anti-Serb graffiti sprayed on the front of the town hall ("a schoolboy prank," Baba had said), and some hand grenades had exploded in a nearby village, but on the whole everything was quiet. Too quiet, perhaps. They all began to believe that the worst was over. After all, what could be worse than the massacre of the seventy members of the Jashari family?

The warmth of spring turned too early into the heat of summer. The ubiquitous crows were squawking over territory and bits of food like old women squabbling in the marketplace. Even with all the windows open, the classroom on that last day of May was stifling. All Meli wanted was to be outdoors—not crowded with fifty other upper-grade children into a room of the house the Albanians used for a school. All the regular schools now belonged to the Serbs.

It was so hot that Meli found herself nodding as Mr. Uka droned on and on. To keep awake, she began to study the teacher's nose. It was so big. It occurred to her that Mr. Uka reminded her of a pelican. He was so patriotic that he should have looked like a proper Kosovar stork, but his nose was bulbous, not long and patrician. Alas, much closer kin to the pelicans she'd seen in books than to a stork. In her boredom, she drew a picture of a pelican that looked surprisingly like Mr. Uka. Zana, who shared her desk, peered over Meli's arm. She began to giggle. It was contagious. Meli couldn't help herself.

"Zana, Meli, come to the front," Mr. Uka ordered.

Meli tried to slip the picture into her pocket, but it was too late. Mr. Uka held out his hand. He studied the picture for a minute. *Don't let him see the resemblance.* "Very clever," he said. "But what do pelicans have to do with the history of Kosovo?"

"Nothing, sir," Meli mumbled. Even with her back to Mehmet, she could feel his disapproval. She didn't dare look. She knew how angry her brother must be.

"Then we will keep the pelican for science class," the teacher said. "And I would like the two of you to stay after school to catch up on history."

When Mr. Uka finally dismissed the girls, Mehmet was nowhere to be seen. *He ran home to tattle on me,* Meli thought. It wasn't fair. Baba would want an explanation as to why Mehmet hadn't waited—why he was letting the girls walk home alone. Baba had told him months ago that he was to look out for them. Their father would be angry with them both.

As always, the girls had to pass the police station on their way. A Serb policeman was loitering outside. "Where are you girls headed?" he asked. He spoke, of course, in Serbian, and Meli had sense enough to answer in the same language. "Just home," she said. The man shrugged. Out of sight of the station the girls walked faster, and once she had left Zana at her house, Meli broke into a run. She was very late.

Yes, there was Baba waiting outside the store. "Meli," he said. "Praise God, you're home. But where is Mehmet?"

TWO

Mehmet Is Missing

BABA'S QUESTION HIT MELI LIKE A BLOW TO HER CHEST. What on earth did he mean?

"Where's Mehmet?" he asked again. "He isn't with you?"

She shook her head, and when she opened her mouth, her voice shook as well. "Mr. Uka made me and Zana stay after dismissal. I—I thought Mehmet would be here already."

Baba didn't ask her why she'd had to stay after school. He would have known it was for punishment, but he seemed not to care. "I told Mehmet to come straight home. I had work for him at the store." He began to pace up and down the street, but when he got to the corner, he stopped himself and came back to where Meli stood. "Come inside. It won't do for us to talk in the street."

There were no customers in the store. Still, Baba led Meli to the back corner. She found herself looking over her shoulder to see if anyone was coming to the door while her father talked. She had never seen him look fearful before, and it frightened her. "What did he say to you?" he asked. "Was he running off to play soccer again?"

"He didn't speak to me after school, Baba. I—I think he was angry because I misbehaved and had to stay late. I thought he was coming right home."

"Tell your mama to come down here."

"Baba. You don't think anything has happened to Mehmet?" Sometimes Albanian men disappeared, but Mehmet was only thirteen. Surely . . .

"Just get your mother. You stay and watch the little ones. And don't frighten them."

She climbed the inside stairs to the apartment. The boys were playing in the garden as usual. Mama was in the kitchen preparing supper, and Vlora was sitting on a high stool pretending to help. Mama looked up when Meli came into the room. "Meli. You children are very late today."

"Baba needs you downstairs for a minute, Mama. Vlora and I will finish making supper, won't we, Vlora?"

Vlora smiled. "I'm making stew," she said.

It was many minutes before Mama came back up the stairs. She was breathing heavily. "Baba's going around to Neshim's," she said. "Those two boys probably got into a soccer game and forgot the time." She came close to Meli standing at the stove. "Try not to worry," she whispered, pushing a strand of hair from Meli's forehead.

How could Meli not worry? Her family lived in a country where people were known to disappear without a trace. Men, mostly—men who were suspected of Kosovo Liberation Army connections. But for all his posturing, Mehmet was only a boy. He wasn't part of the KLA. Surely not even a Serb policeman would think . . . But who knew what those people thought?

Mama fed the youngsters early. When Isuf asked where Baba and Mehmet were, Mama just said, "Oh, Baba and Mehmet had some errands to run. They'll eat when they get home."

Meli couldn't believe how calm her mother sounded. Her own stomach was churning like an eggbeater.

Bedtime came for the young ones, and still no Baba or Mehmet. Meli tried to do her homework, though none of the math problems made sense and she soon gave up. She couldn't make her head work properly. Everything jumped about inside. She flipped on the television, but all the blare of Serbian propaganda just made her more nervous, and she switched it off and went to the front window to watch for them. Finally, she saw a figure emerge from the shadows. Surely it was Baba, although the man walking up the dark street was bent over like a ninety-year-old. She must go meet him. She had to hear his news, however terrible it was. She started toward the door, but Mama caught her arm. "Wait, Meli. It is better if we talk inside," she said.

Baba came through the side gate and up the stairs so slowly that Meli thought she might cry out before he actually reached the landing. In the light from the kitchen his face looked gray.

"No word?" Mama asked as she opened the door. It was more of a statement than a question.

Baba shook his head, sighing deeply as he took off his shoes at the door. He stumbled through into the living room and fell into a chair. "Neshim said he spoke to Mehmet after school." He went on, careful not to look at Meli. "He was angry, Neshim said, and not sure what he should do. He knew he was supposed to walk home with the girls, but he had promised to help me, so finally he just said he had to go and ran ahead." Baba sighed again. "That was the last Neshim saw of him—running up the street."

"What of his other friends?" Mama asked. "The other boys he plays soccer with. Surely someone saw him after that."

"I went from house to house. None of the boys know anything." The look that passed between her parents sent ice through Meli's whole body.

"I'm sure he's all right," Meli said. "He has to be." The words were hardly out of her mouth before she knew how foolish and desperate she sounded.

"*Inshallah,*" murmured Mama.

Inshallah. God willing. *Yes, please, God,* Meli prayed. *Let him be safe.*

"You must eat some supper, Hashim," Mama said. "It's very late."

Her father shook his head. "How can I eat when my first-born is missing and I don't know where he is to be found?" He lurched to his feet. "We will both be home soon. *Inshallah.*"

"Hashim. Where are you going?"

"To the police," Baba said.

"No, not the police."

"They are the only ones who know where my son is. You know that is true, Sevdie." He walked out the door, leaving it open behind him.

"Go with him, Meli," Mama said. "Perhaps they won't arrest him if he has his daughter with him."

Her father soon realized that Meli was following him up the street. "Go home, child," he said. "Stay with your mother. She's already anxious about your brother. I don't want her to have to worry about you as well."

Meli just shook her head. As scared as she was, she was determined to do as Mama had asked. The police had seen her walk past every day with Mehmet. They might remember that the two of them were only schoolchildren, not terrorists to be jailed . . . or tortured . . . or . . . killed. She closed her eyes to shut out such thoughts.

The station door was locked. Her father knocked, and when nobody answered, he beat on the heavy wooden door with his fist.

"No, Baba," Meli begged. "You'll make them angry."

He ignored her and kept right on beating until the door opened wide enough for a pistol to stick out through the crack. "What do you want?" a voice demanded in Serbian.

"I need your help," Baba said meekly, as though he really believed a Serb policeman would help an Albanian. "My son never returned home from school today."

"So? Can I help it if your boy has run away?"

Baba stuck his big hand in the crack and forced it open wider, ignoring the pistol in the officer's hand. Watching, Meli could hardly breathe. "I think one of your men has made a mistake. My son is only a schoolboy. He knows nothing of politics." It was a lie. Mehmet knew plenty about politics, but of course what her father meant was that Mehmet was not a part of the KLA.

"Who are you?"

"My name is Hashim Lleshi. I own a small grocery store on the west side of town. This is my daughter, Meli. My son, Mehmet, who is missing, is only thirteen. He—is he here? Do you have him in custody? By mistake? Perhaps you have confused him with someone else?"

"Come back in the morning if you have a question."

"But to make a child spend the night in jail . . . He . . . Do you have children?" Baba's voice was low and pleading now. It hurt Meli to hear him humiliate himself before this Serb, but she knew he was determined to do whatever it took to get Mehmet safely home.

"I said, come back in the morning!" The policeman poked her father with the pistol to force him out of the doorway. "And be glad I didn't arrest you."

"Come on, Baba," Meli whispered.

Reluctantly, her father backed away. Once again he became the old man Meli had seen coming up the street. "Pray for your brother, Meli," he said. They were the only words he spoke during the long walk home. She did pray, or tried to; they were not a family who practiced daily prayers. As they walked past the dark shadow of the mosque, she prayed that God would not hold their lack of piety against them. Surely he wouldn't. God was the all-merciful, wasn't he?

Baba and Meli went back to the station the next morning, but the result was the same. The Serbian police would not even say if Mehmet was in the jail or not.

❋ ❋ ❋

In the weeks following Mehmet's disappearance, the family went through the motions of getting up in the morning, eating, working, and lying down to sleepless nights. Meli couldn't make herself go to school, and her parents didn't seem to have the energy to insist. Suppose something should happen while she was at school? It didn't make sense, but somehow she reckoned that since she had been the cause of her brother's disappearance, she had to be home to make him come back safely. Whenever she wasn't working in the store or helping Mama with housework, she was standing at the front window, straining to see Mehmet turning the corner, coming down the side street, walking through the gate, climbing the stairs. He was laughing as he took off his shoes and came into the apartment.

Sometimes she changed the picture in her mind. This time Mehmet was walking down the street, opening the door of the shop. She imagined the bell ringing to announce his entrance, and Baba rushing forward to embrace him. . . .

Meli rehearsed these scenes day after day, time after time.

Once, as she stood at the window, Mama came over and put her arm around her daughter's shoulders.

"It won't bring him home sooner," Mama said gently.

But it might. If only I stare long enough and hard enough, I can will him home. In part of her mind Meli knew this was foolishness, but she couldn't seem to help herself. It was guilt that drove her. If only she had behaved that day in school, Mehmet would be home now, teasing her, lording it over her.

Zana had called the very first day to ask why she hadn't come by, why she and Mehmet had missed school. "What's the matter, Meli? Are you both sick?"

"No, not exactly. It's . . . it's . . . I can't talk about it on the phone."

But even when Zana came to the apartment, Meli could only say, "Mehmet is missing. We don't know anything."

Zana had hugged her, but Meli hadn't been able to cry. She couldn't even say, *It's all my fault!* The words stuck like burrs in her dry throat.

❋ ❋ ❋

Meli turned twelve in June. Mama made a little cake, but no one felt like celebrating. Still no word. And then one evening, when she wasn't even looking, Mehmet appeared. At first when Meli saw him in the doorway, she couldn't believe it was him. He was so thin. Besides, he had knocked on the kitchen door. When had Mehmet ever knocked on his own door?

"Mehmet?"

The ghost-like figure nodded. "Not a pelican," he said, stepping out of his shoes—or what was left of them.

Meli reached out and pulled her brother over the threshold.

18

"Mama! Baba! It's Mehmet. He's come home!" She tried not to stare at his thin face as he bent to take off what was left of his once-shiny shoes, but she couldn't help herself.

Mama came running from the bedroom, nearly knocking Meli to the floor as she threw her arms around her son. "My Mehmet!" she cried. "Oh, my Mehmet." She led him to a chair and sat him down. "I have goulash," she said. "You must be hungry. Go get Baba, Meli. He must see his firstborn."

The family just stood and watched as Mehmet ate the goulash Mama heated up for him. The little boys pressed themselves against their brother's chair while Vlora jumped up and down with joy, but Meli and her parents were standing, staring at Mehmet as though he would disappear if they took their eyes from him. Occasionally, Baba would touch Mehmet's shoulder, as though making sure his son was still there. Their heads were crowded with questions, but no one knew what to ask or how to begin asking.

It was, as usual, Mehmet who spoke first. "The bastards beat me up and then took me out to the countryside and dumped me." He paused for a long time, looking down at his empty bowl. Nobody moved. "I guess they thought they'd killed me."

A little cry escaped Mama's lips. Her hand flew to her mouth.

"But I wasn't dead." Mehmet gave a short, bitter laugh. "Some KLA men found me. They took care of me until I was well. I wanted to stay with them, help them kill those devils, but . . . but they made me come home."

"Thank God," Baba whispered.

"They said I must tell you Uncle Fadil was right," he said. "We can't stay here. We have to leave as soon as possible."

THREE

Leaving Home

BABA CALLED A COUSIN WHO LIVED ON THE OTHER SIDE of town to come look after the shop in the Lleshis' absence. No one in his family had tangled with the police. They had no reason to flee. The cousin was overjoyed. He came immediately for the extra keys to the store and the apartment. His family would move in the very next day. Perhaps it was unreasonable, but his delight angered Meli. The cousin was a lazy man who had never in his entire life worked as hard as Baba did in a single day. It wasn't fair that he should have their nice apartment and all the food in the store for nothing—even if for only a few weeks.

There was no telephone at the farm, so as soon as the matter was settled with his cousin, Baba got on his bicycle and rode out to the country. It was almost dusk when he returned in the Lada with Uncle Fadil. Although Uncle Fadil kept insisting that there was plenty of food at the farm, Mama and Baba were determined not to be any more of a burden than necessary. The men and Mehmet loaded the back of the car with fifty-pound sacks of flour, cases of cooking oil, sacks of onions and potatoes, big cans of white cheese, some jars of honey and plum jam, and a box of assorted canned goods: the goulash that Mehmet liked and the *pashteta* that Baba liked to spread on his bread in the morning. Thick coils of spicy sausage almost masked the usual smells of the old car. Space, though hardly enough, was left just behind the front seat for the four older children. The family was ready—or as ready as they could be—to leave the only home the children had ever known, with no idea of when they would see it again.

"Wait," said Mama, as Meli was about to climb over the front seat into the tiny space behind it. "My photo—my parents' photo!"

Meli took the key from Baba and ran back up the outside stairs. Out of habit she slipped off her shoes at the door and raced into the living room. Her hands were shaking as she took the picture down from its special place atop the television set. The grandparents she had never known stared out at her as though wondering why they must leave their comfortable setting. She got a towel from the bathroom and wrapped the picture in it to protect the glass. *Don't drop it!* she told her shaking hands as she stuffed her feet into her shoes and, the precious picture tucked under her arm, closed and locked the door behind her. Slowly, she descended the steps, went out the gate, and returned to the waiting family.

She didn't look back. She hadn't said good-bye to her room, or the kitchen, or the living room. She hadn't said good-bye to her school, or even to Zana, who would never understand how she could leave without a word. But she wouldn't cry. *We must all be brave*, she kept telling herself. *Besides, we'll be back soon. Of course we will.* But something echoed deep and dark inside her stomach: *Inshallah.* God willing.

Mama, Baba, and Vlora were crowded into the front seat of the car with Uncle Fadil. Meli, Mehmet, Isuf, and Adil were in the rear. They sat facing backwards, their spines slammed against the front seat, their knees drawn up against their chests, surrounded by what were for now the family belongings. Mama had insisted that they bring their winter jackets and a blanket for everyone. It was summertime; surely they'd be home before anyone needed a jacket. Although Auntie Burbuqe had plenty of utensils for cooking and eating, there were some Mama couldn't bear to leave behind for the careless cousins to misuse. No furniture, of course—the foodstuffs were the important cargo. Vlora had been allowed one doll, but there were no other toys in the car. They had left so much behind, but at least Mama had her parents' photograph. It was the only thing she had to remind her of her childhood home.

"You look like my mother," Mama had often said to Meli. "She was such a beautiful woman. See, in the photo? You can tell how beautiful she was." And Meli would obediently look at the photo and agree, though her grandmother seemed stiff and plain to her, and she secretly hoped she would be much prettier than that when she grew up.

Now Meli strained for a last sight of home in the fading light. It was a lovely place, her town, on the banks of the Drin River, nestled between the hills that divided Kosovo right down the middle and the snowcapped Cursed Mountains, which barred the way to Albania, from where in the mists of the long-ago past her ancestors had made their way to this fertile plain.

But the beauty of the sights she was leaving behind was soon crowded out by a riot of fears. She was afraid that they would be stopped by a police patrol, or worse, by Serb paramilitaries, who had begun to act as though they were more powerful than the police. If the Lleshis were stopped, they would be searched. Not that the family owned any guns—Baba didn't believe in guns—but who knew what the Serbs might find suspicious? Suppose they just took Baba or Mehmet or Uncle Fadil away for no reason at all? Mehmet had disappeared once already, probably just because a boy running down the street past the police station had aroused their suspicion. Maybe, now that he had been jailed and beaten and had lived with the guerrillas, he was on some secret list of KLA sympathizers. That must be it—that was why he had insisted that they leave town. She shuddered.

"Mehmet." She was whispering so as not to wake up the little boys, who had fallen asleep. Those in front wouldn't be able to hear her over the racket of the engine. "Mehmet, if we're stopped, you have to hide."

Mehmet gave a snort. "Where? Among the sausages?"

Yes, it would be foolish to try to hide. She fought to keep alert, to keep her eyes open for the first signs of danger. But she was tired. The next thing she knew, the car had rattled to a stop. She straightened up quickly. Where were they? To her relief she made out in the darkness the outline of the family farmhouse. Mehmet was still sitting as stiff as a board against the back of the front seat, his eyes wide open. He hadn't fallen asleep—she was sure of it.

The adults got out of the car, Baba carrying the sleeping Vlora. Mehmet clambered over the front seat and out the door. Meli tried to stretch out her numb legs in the small space he had left and was about to wake her little brothers when Auntie Burbuqe came hurrying out of the house, carrying a bag.

Even in the pale light from the doorway Meli could see how agitated she was. She said something to Uncle Fadil, who in turn spoke softly to his brother. Baba shook his head. Then Mehmet went over and talked with Baba. Now Auntie Burbuqe was handing the large bag to Mama. No, she shouldn't wake Isuf and Adil—not yet. Isuf had fallen against her, so Meli sat still, but she craned her neck, trying desperately to figure out what was happening. Finally, Mehmet climbed back over the seat into the space she made for him by gently prodding Isuf to a sitting position. "What is it?" Meli asked. "What's the matter?"

Mehmet didn't answer. He waited until Uncle Fadil took his place behind the wheel again, and Mama, carrying the bag Auntie had given her, and Baba, with Vlora still in his arms, struggled back into the front seat. "It's not safe here," he said. "We have to go."

"What did Auntie Burbuqe say?"

Mehmet pushed Isuf gently to give himself a bit more room. Isuf mumbled something in his sleep. Adil stirred and nestled closer to Meli's shoulder.

"Shh," Mehmet said. "Don't wake them up. We have miles to go. The longer they sleep, the better."

"But why can't we stay here?"

"It's not safe."

It was all he would say. Sometimes Mehmet could be so maddening. "Why not?" Meli demanded.

"Shh. There are paramilitaries all around. They've been threatening everyone—telling them to leave the country."

"Leave?" How could those thugs order them to leave their own land? "But what about Auntie Burbuqe and Granny?"

"I don't know," he whispered. "Maybe Uncle Fadil will come back for them later. Or—or maybe they'll be safe if I'm not around." He said the last bitterly.

"You don't know that!"

"Quiet, Meli," he said, putting his hand over her mouth. "I know because Auntie Burbuqe as much as said so. I think they know someone who knows someone—you know how it goes."

She didn't know. She shook away his hand. "What are you talking about, Mehmet?"

"Shh. Forget it. Information is dangerous. People get killed for it."

She shut up then. But who had gotten word to Auntie Burbuqe? How did she know things they didn't? She tried not to think about it. She tried to be glad simply that she was with her family, that Mehmet was there beside her. Whatever the danger, it felt safer for them to be all together.

It was too dark to see where the car was going; they were traveling without headlights for the first part of the trip. Even so, Meli knew the bumpy road was winding up and up. "Where are we going, Mehmet?"

"Into the hills," he answered. In the strange night, even his voice sounded dark.

"To our grazing lands?" Years ago the family used to take sheep and goats to their ancestral lands in the hills for the summer. But they hadn't done that for years. "I hope that old shack is still standing."

"We're not going to our place."

"Then where?"

"Somewhere else. Farther south."

"But there's no one up there we know."

"There's the KLA."

A chill went through her. "But we don't belong to the KLA."

"They'll protect us."

She was shivering all over now. How could Mehmet be sure? A little band of KLA had saved his life—she knew that—but did that mean all of them were kind? The KLA might be patriots and heroes, but they were fighters, desperate ones, and safe only in children's war play, not in the dark hills they hid among. She had heard it whispered that if the KLA suspected that you were a spy or even a government sympathizer, they would kill you as fast as the Serbs would.

"Don't be afraid, Meli. It's all right." Mehmet was reading her mind. "Besides, we don't have much choice, do we?"

The car spiraled higher and higher into the darkness. She could smell the chill mountain air. Uncle Fadil had put on the dim parking lights, but Meli was riding backward in the over-packed car, and nothing was really visible. She was afraid she might vomit, either from car sickness, the car's strange mixture of smells, or fear, she couldn't be sure. *I can't throw up,* she told herself. *I have to be strong.* Besides, there was no way to move herself over to the half-open window to throw up—she would wake the little boys, and she couldn't do that. They were sleeping so peacefully.

"Mehmet," she whispered. "When will we get there?"

She sensed rather than saw Mehmet shrug.

Her face was hot and feverish, but her arms, sticking out of her light summer dress, were covered with goose bumps. It had gotten much cooler as they climbed. Her winter jacket was stuffed somewhere near the rear hatch. She wished she could jerk out one of the blankets they were sitting on to put around her shoulders, but even if it were possible, she wouldn't dare. Questions tumbled over in her mind like laundry in their old washing machine. *Where will we sleep tonight? On the ground? How will we cook or bathe or go to the toilet?* The only houses in the hills were the summer shacks of goat and sheep herders, flimsy structures perched on ancestral grazing lands. Her whole body ached for her own comfortable bed and her cozy home. *Stop it!* She rubbed her arms to warm them.

Once more Mehmet seemed to read her mind. "There are

camps up there. It won't be like home, but there'll be shelter. I promise."

How could Mehmet promise anything? How would he know how the KLA lived? She didn't dare ask. She didn't want information that could be dangerous—especially not from her brother.

The Lada stopped so suddenly that the four of them were thrown hard against the seat. Adil gave a startled cry.

"Hush," Mehmet said. There was a mumble of voices. He was trying to listen, to find out what was happening. "I think we're almost there," he whispered.

Just then the beams of two powerful flashlights lit the darkness. Both little boys were awake now. "What's the matter? What happened?" Isuf asked.

"Hush," Meli said.

The dark figure of a man went around the hood of the car to the driver's window, and another went to the rear side window and peered in at the children and then to the back and opened the hatch. The beam of the flashlight raked their faces and the contents of the car. The four of them sat there, as though frozen in place.

"It's only food and children back here. Let them pass," he called to his companion, and slammed shut the hatch. For once Mehmet didn't protest at being called a child.

Uncle Fadil ground the gears and gunned the engine. Climbing across Isuf, Mehmet shoved aside a sack of flour and a can of cheese to roll down the window. He poked his head out, staring ahead as the car wound farther up into the hills, now with its headlights illuminating the way. "I can see campfires," he said excitedly. "We're almost there."

FOUR

Camping

THE LADA JERKED TO A STOP. AS SOON AS THE FRONT OF the car emptied, Mehmet clambered over the seat and jumped out. The little boys had fallen asleep again. Meli shook them gently. "Wake up, Isuf, Adil; we're there," she said, having no idea where "there" might be.

Both boys shifted as if to shake off her hands, but they didn't open their eyes. *It must be wonderful to sleep like that.* She envied them. They had missed all the anxiety. At six and eight, they didn't seem to realize how dangerous their world had become.

Baba was calling to her.

"They won't wake up," Meli said.

"Well, let them sleep while we unload," Baba said. "I'll open the back. Can you push things toward us, or do you want Mehmet to help?"

"I can do it," she said. She wanted Baba to know that she was going to be one of the grown-ups, one of the strong ones. She shifted to her knees, and when Mehmet and the men had unloaded what they could easily reach, she began to push a heavy sack of flour toward the hatch. It wasn't as easy as she thought. Mehmet quickly became impatient and climbed in to help. With the four of them working, it didn't take long to unload, maybe ten minutes or so. She crawled back to the boys and shook them hard enough this time to wake them up.

"Are we at Uncle Fadil's house already?" Adil asked sleepily, blinking his eyes.

"No," she said. "Baba changed his mind. We're not staying with Uncle Fadil after all. We're . . . we're camping out."

"Oh, good!" said Isuf, wide awake now. "Like a real army. Just like the KLA!"

"Yes," she said. "Just like that."

There was, as Mehmet had promised, a tent, but it was hardly big enough for three people, much less seven with their belongings.

Uncle Fadil was closing the hatch, obviously anxious to get moving while it was still dark. They gathered around him to say good-bye. "When will you bring Burbuqe and Granny?" Mama asked.

Uncle Fadil shook his head. "Mother is so old," he said. "Maybe it's better we stay and take our chances. At least she has a bed to sleep in."

How could they argue? Meli hugged her uncle. Mehmet and Baba shook his hand. "Thank you, brother," Baba said. "We'll see you soon, *inshallah*."

"*Inshallah*," Uncle Fadil echoed. "May we see one another well," he added as he climbed into the car.

"May your life be lengthened," Baba said. The formal words of parting hung in the night air like black clouds before a storm. They stood without another word, listening to the fading noise of the beloved old Lada and watching its dim rear lights until they disappeared beyond the first curve.

❋ ❋ ❋

In the morning they could see their camping place. Another tent stood not far from their own. The plain where the two tents were pitched was partly surrounded by chestnut trees, and a stream flowed from above the camp and ran past it. Down the hill a bit, a dilapidated shack straddled the stream. No one needed to tell Meli that the old shack would be their toilet while they lived here. In the days when they had gone to the family's grazing lands, they had often used just such an outhouse.

Mama found a bag with a loaf of bread brought from home and gave each child a piece topped by a bit of cheese while Baba and Mehmet chose a spot in front of the tent where Mama could make a fire. As they worked, a gray-haired man emerged from the woods carrying an armload of firewood.

"Please," he said, when he saw them. "Use this for your fire today."

"I worship your honor," Baba said gratefully.

"May *you* be with honor," their new neighbor replied.

He was a sad-faced man, Meli thought, but very kind. Perhaps a few days here wouldn't be too awful. She turned to see that Mama had dug out her old mixing bowl and a spoon.

Mama smiled at her. "Last night Auntie Burbuqe gave us all the right ingredients, so I think today is a good day to make *flija*," she said.

"*Flija!*" Isuf yelled, and he and Adil and Vlora crowded so close to their mother that she could hardly beat the thin batter.

As soon as the coals were ready, Mama poured a layer of batter into the big round metal pan, put the lid on, and covered the lid with coals.

"When can we eat it?" Vlora asked.

"It takes hours," Isuf said with big-brother importance. "You have to be very patient."

"But I'm hungry now," his little sister protested.

"Everybody wants *flija* now," said their father, "but it doesn't hurry for anybody. Now go help Mehmet find more firewood while you wait."

When the first layer was cooked, Mama took a forked stick and carefully lifted the lid of the pan, added another layer of batter, replaced the lid and the coals, and then sat back to wait until this layer was done. Each time the lid was taken off, one of the children rushed up to see if it was time to eat, but it never was—not until the middle of the day, when the many-layered *flija* was finally fat and brown. Mama cut two pieces and put them on a plate with a bit of the precious jam. "Take these to our new neighbors, Meli, to thank them."

❈ ❈ ❈

With cheese and Mama's *flija* topped with honey, that first full meal at the hillside camp felt a bit like a celebration, but as the days wore on, there was very little to celebrate. So much they had always taken for granted was missing—electricity, a proper stove, a washing machine, running water, an indoor toilet. The fresh eggs and butter and milk that Auntie Burbuqe had given them were quickly gone. Each morning, while Meli and Mama went out to fetch water from the stream, Mehmet and Baba gathered sticks for the next day's fire. Their new neighbor had advised this: They should never let themselves run out of firewood, he had said. "And don't let the children wander too far up that way," he had added, waving toward the top of the hill. "That's where the military camp is. It's off-limits." *So that's where the KLA hide themselves.* It was a thought that both thrilled Meli and frightened her.

"Do you have children?" Baba had asked the man that first morning. It was simply politeness speaking, but the man stiffened. "I had two sons. The elder, Visar, was slaughtered before my eyes, and the younger . . ." He paused. "Someday he will come home again. *Inshallah*."

Baba had touched his chest in the traditional gesture of sympathy. "May the Lord leave you healthy," he had said.

"May you be healthy," the grieved father had answered, and sighed deeply. "God wrote it in his book before any of us were born. What can we do? We must reconcile ourselves to it."

Reconcile yourself to your son's murder? How was that possible? If Mehmet had died, would any of them ever have been able to reconcile themselves, Meli wondered. As for the neighbor's second son, was he in these hills—or some other hills—plotting vengeance for his brother's death? No one asked that question.

Each morning when they came out of their tent, they could see that other families had come to join the makeshift camp. There were no more proper tents, so the new arrivals had to make do with plastic sheets hung over chestnut tree branches and propped up with sticks. It made the Lleshis' crowded tent seem almost luxurious. Every day Meli hoped that a car coming up the steep, curving road would bring Zana, or someone she knew from her old school, but they were all strangers.

"How do you stand it up here?" a new girl asked her one day. Looking at her clothes, Meli realized that the newcomer was used to a much more comfortable life than even the Lleshis had known. She felt a pang of pity for the girl, her clothes not yet stained and torn, her face untanned.

"I try to pretend I'm on vacation," Meli said. "If the family is on a camping trip, everyone thinks it's fun to fetch water and cook over an open fire, don't you think?"

The girl sneered. "I'm *not* on vacation," she said. "And it's *not* fun. Though maybe for you villagers . . ."

Meli didn't reply, but she wished she could tell Zana: That girl didn't even have a tent to sleep in, but she thought she was better than me because her father wasn't born on a farm.

There were advantages to never having been rich, Meli decided. Though, at that moment, having a bed and a roof and warm water to bathe in seemed like the height of luxury.

❊ ❊ ❊

The KLA soldiers who appeared through the woods almost daily to inspect the family camp didn't look like much of an army to Meli. They wore ragged clothes with a makeshift double-eagle insignia sewn on the back, and they carried ancient guns, which Mehmet identified as cast-off Chinese or Russian weapons, some of them dating back to the fifties. "It was better at my other camp," he said. "They had weapons smuggled in from America." Meli found that hard to believe, but she didn't try to argue. Like everyone else in the hill camp, the soldiers had trouble keeping clean. Baba's once handsome mustache was now just the top of a scraggly beard. All of the men grew beards, because that was easier than trying to shave. Mehmet couldn't have grown a beard to save his life, but, like the older boys who could, he hung around with the soldiers as much as possible.

It seemed to Meli that the soldiers regarded Mehmet as a sort of pet. They gave him an old gypsy stove—"so your mama can bake you bread and make you strong." The Lleshis rejoiced over that old iron stove, Mama most of all. It was an iron box with one side for the fire and the other for an oven. You could make soup or stew on top, or boil coffee—if you had any. Mehmet walked around like a farmyard cock, he was so proud of "his" stove.

Then one day Meli discovered that one of the soldiers had

loaned Mehmet his rifle and had taken him into the woods to teach him how to shoot.

"Baba will be angry," she said to him later. "You know how he feels about guns."

Mehmet shrugged. "Baba is the only man I know who hates guns. Someone needs to learn how to defend our family," he said. "And our country."

"Don't even think of joining up," she said. "You're only a beardless boy."

"Once you've been in jail, you're not a kid anymore," he replied, the words sending a chill up his sister's spine. He was no longer the brother she thought she knew. He didn't speak about that terrible time, but it had changed him. He was harder, and he rarely joked or played with his little brothers. Despite his squawky voice and smooth cheeks, Meli knew that he was becoming a man—not the sort of kind, loving man that Baba was, but a secretive man with the sharp and watchful eyes of a blackbird.

So it was a relief to Meli when she realized that no one from the KLA had been around for several days. "They're fighting down below," Mehmet told her. After several weeks the rumor spread around the family camp that there was only a handful of fighters left in the hills. Down on the plains the KLA were waging a major campaign. "We're winning!" Mehmet said. At first that seemed to be true, but by the end of August word came to the camp that President Milosević had launched another offensive. Serbian soldiers were pouring over the border from the north. Before long, the KLA fighters began to come straggling back up the hill, many of them wounded. The soldier who had loaned Mehmet his rifle for practice was among those who never returned.

※ ※ ※

On the hillsides the chestnut flowers had turned into burrs. Before long they would pop open to reveal the nuts they protected, and it would be fully autumn. The days grew shorter and the nights colder. The Lleshis had brought jackets and blankets, but still they shivered. In some ways it was lucky that the tent was so small. They had to sleep close together, which kept them warm. Meli liked the feeling of having her family huddled close. Not only were the younger children's bodies like little stoves, but they slept so peacefully that it helped her relax and fall asleep herself. Mehmet always took the place by the tent flap, a little apart from the rest. Sometimes Meli would wake in the night to see him sitting bolt upright, as though listening. One night in early September, she woke up with the strange sensation that something was wrong. She sat up and looked around. Mehmet was gone.

Meli's first thought was to wake up her father and tell him that Mehmet was missing. But for once Baba was sleeping soundly, and she couldn't bear to wake him only to give him bad news. Besides, Mehmet had probably just gone to the outhouse. She was worrying for nothing. That was it. She was just being her usual anxious self.

She lay down again. Adil snuggled closer. *If it's this cold in September, whatever will we do come winter?* She turned so she could hear any movement of the tent flap. Whenever she heard the tiniest *blap blap*, she stiffened, willing Mehmet to come in and lie down, but each time it was only the wind.

Finally, she couldn't hold still another second. She carefully lifted herself over Adil, one knee at a time, and felt the ground cloth along the flap. Then she began to paw frantically along the front of the tent. *Mehmet has taken his blanket.* She covered her mouth to keep from calling out and crawled through the flap of the tent to stand up outside in the chilled night air.

She felt for her own shoes among the pile of family shoes before the tent. The cooler nights demanded that they all sleep in their clothes, which was a good thing. It meant she could scout around and try to find her brother before the rest of the family knew he was missing. She was sure that if Mehmet had told their parents he was leaving, he wouldn't have sneaked out in the middle of the night.

Fortunately, there was enough moonlight for her to see her way around the makeshift shelters in the family encampment. Mehmet wouldn't be in one of those, she was sure. She took a deep breath and headed up through the trees toward the campfires of the KLA. She hadn't gone very far before she felt cold metal poking into her backbone. A flashlight shone in her face, blinding her. "It's only a little girl," a man's rough voice said, and then asked, "Where are you going in the middle of the night, child? Did you miss your way to the toilet?"

"I'm looking for my brother." She couldn't help the quaver in her voice, even though she told herself that the fighters wouldn't hurt her. Indeed, the gun was no longer on her back.

"How old is your brother?" the voice behind her asked.

"Thirteen."

"Oh," said the voice. "I thought you meant *little* brother. Don't worry. Your brother can take care of himself. Now go back to your tent like a good girl and don't go prowling around where you don't belong."

"His—his name is Mehmet Lleshi. If you see him, will you tell him his family . . . his family is anxious about him?"

The flashlight was lowered, and the voice behind it said gently, "Really, there's no need to worry. Your brother is fine, I'm sure. Go on back now, child, and get some sleep."

It was useless to argue. She turned back toward the family encampment and crept into the tent. Isuf and Adil had rolled over against each other. She pushed them apart as gently as she could and lay down again between them.

"Meli?" Of course Mama would wake up.

"It's all right, Mama. I just went out to—to relieve myself." She heard her mother roll over, grunting a bit as she did so.

It was impossible to fall asleep again. She tried to keep from tossing and turning in the narrow wedge between her brothers. The night stretched on and on, until at last morning pierced the cracks around the tent flap and surrounded the canvas with its weak warmth.

Baba cleared his throat, got to his feet, and—hunched over so that he wouldn't brush the top of the tent—stepped carefully over Isuf, Meli, and Adil, pausing briefly at the empty spot that should have been Mehmet. Then he raised the flap and went outdoors. Meli got up and followed him out.

"Mehmet's gone," she said.

"So I see," he said.

"He took his blanket."

Baba nodded. "Tell your mother to start the fire and feed you. As soon as I gather the firewood, I'll go look for him."

Everyone wanted to know where Baba and Mehmet were, but Meli just told them that Baba had said they were not to wait with breakfast, that the two of them would be back soon. Mama gave her a questioning look, but Meli just shook her head.

It was a quiet meal, and because there was not much to eat, it was over quickly. Meli left the cleaning up to Mama and took the pot to the stream for water. They always needed more water, and if she was alone she wouldn't have to deal with any more unanswerable questions.

It was midmorning before Baba returned, a glum-faced Mehmet trailing several steps behind. At least Mehmet had enough respect for Baba not to defy him, Meli thought. That was a relief.

She didn't speak of his disappearance until later that afternoon, when she found Mehmet sitting under a chestnut tree at the far edge of the camp. He was ripping up little clumps of grass and pitching them down the hill. He didn't even glance at her when she sat down beside him. She had practiced in her head several things to say, but finally she simply blurted out, "I'm glad you're back."

"When I'm fifteen I'll join up, no matter what Baba says."

She hadn't practiced an answer to that, so she said nothing and comforted herself with the knowledge that it would be more than a year before her brother turned fifteen. Surely the war would be long over by then.

❋ ❋ ❋

Meli slept hard that night, untroubled by the anxieties of the night before, but when she left the tent in the morning, she saw only Mehmet coming from the trees carrying firewood. "Where's Baba?" she asked.

Mehmet shrugged. "I don't know. He was gone when I woke up. Mama said he left the message that I was to be in charge, so you're going to have to listen to me for a change." He sounded almost like her bossy older brother again. "It's past time to eat. Where's Mama? Why doesn't she have the fire made already?"

Meli went looking for their mother and found her trying, as

cold as it was, to wash herself behind the tent. Mama was such a modest woman; it must be humiliating for her to have such little privacy. Indeed, when she saw Meli, she blushed and began hastily to pull her dress on over her undergarments.

"Excuse me, Mama, but I have to know where Baba's gone." It was too much to bear, first losing Mehmet, now her father.

"Shh. He's gone to fetch Uncle Fadil."

"But it's miles—"

"He got a ride partway." She buttoned her dress and put on her big sweater and then her overcoat. "We've got to leave here, Meli," she said quietly. "Before we lose your brother."

FIVE

A School in the Hills

W ITH BABA GONE, THERE WAS MUCH MORE WORK FOR the rest of the family. Everyone missed him. When Adil or Vlora asked about him, Mama would say something like, "Well, a good son has to visit his old mother, you know."

Meli realized that she was the only other person who knew the real reason Baba was gone: to fetch Uncle Fadil and his car to take them all back. She didn't know, of course, where "back" was anymore—back home, where the police might arrest Mehmet again? Or back to the family farm, which was probably already crowded with Uncle Fadil's own daughter and grandchildren?

But anywhere, she told herself, would be warmer than these hills. At least they were not farther up. The mountain heights above them were covered with snow now, and below the alpine meadows and evergreens the leaves of the great beech trees had turned to gold. Mama made everyone sleep so close together that Meli spent every night with someone's foot in her mouth or fist in her eye, and the younger children still cried out from the cold. At first Mehmet objected. It offended his "dignity as a man" to curl up against his siblings like a puppy in a litter, but as it got colder, he stopped complaining.

As she lay awake every night, shivering, praying for sleep to come, she imagined she could hear the rattle of Uncle Fadil's Lada. But then the sound would turn out to be one of the old cars used by the KLA, or the arrival of another family seeking refuge—or just her imagination. It was never Baba coming back.

Summer seemed a distant dream. The chestnuts were ripe now, and she had eaten so many she felt as though she might turn into one. But when they were gone, it would be winter in the foothills as well as up on the mountains. Meli kept thinking longingly of home, of the old house that had been school, and of her friends, especially Zana. There was an old saying: "You never really know someone till you've eaten a sack of salt together." Zana and she were too young to have eaten that much salt, that many meals together, but they had shared so much— their worries about school, about growing up—as, she supposed, girls anywhere might. Over and above these ordinary thoughts, they had agonized about their land and its people. What was to become of them if the Serbs kept pressing them down? It had been a comfort to talk to each other about their fears without any adult seeking to quiet them. More than the shared fears, though, there was the shared laughter. Even when the world about them was grim, they could always find something to giggle about.

But whenever she thought of Zana, she couldn't help but remember that horrible day when the two of them had misbehaved, causing Mehmet to disappear. *If I had just not drawn that stupid picture of Mr. Uka looking like a pelican, Mehmet wouldn't have been arrested, and we would all be warm and safe in our own beds right now.*

The hills were filling up with families who had fled cities and towns below. Surely *their* being here was not all her fault. Indeed, each family seemed to have its own reasons for hiding in the camp, none of which had anything to do with her. She tried to comfort herself, blaming everything on Milosević and the Serbs, who wanted to get rid of everyone in Kosovo who wasn't Serbian, even though the Albanian Kosovars far outnumbered the Serbian ones. She had been born into a Kosovo that had, if not true independence, at least a degree of self-government as part of Yugoslavia. Baba, peace-loving Baba, had served his term in the Yugoslav army. Then Slobodan Milosević came to power, and he took away whatever independence the Kosovars had enjoyed under Tito. *Milosević is scared of us. There are too many Albanians poor and out of work in Kosovo. He sent his army and police down from Serbia to keep us under control. Yes, it's not my fault; it's his fault that we are here in the hills, cold and running out of food.* There were terrifying reports now of whole villages being slaughtered by the Serbian security forces, and rumors that the United Nations would soon be involved.

"Why don't the Americans help us?" she asked Mehmet. Despite Mama's disapproval, every day Mehmet would sneak over to the military camp and get the news. The KLA had a shortwave radio. If Meli wanted to know what was going on, she had to ask her brother. "I thought you said that the Americans were going to help us."

He made a rude noise with his mouth. "The Americans won't do anything. They're too busy trying to get rid of their president to pay attention to *us*."

❄ ❄ ❄

Then one cold morning Mama made everything a little better. She had taken from her dwindling stores the last can of goulash. Meli's mouth watered as she watched Mama's strong fingers rip open the tab and plop the contents into the pot on the stove. When it was warm, Mama handed a spoon and the whole potful to Mehmet. He gobbled it down like a starved puppy. *He might have shared* was Meli's first thought, and then she realized that Mama was up to something.

The flour for making bread was almost gone, so for the rest of them Mama was making a sort of gruel from pounded chestnuts on the gypsy stove. As she stirred this strange concoction, she said, "Mehmet, I think you should start a school for the younger children. All they do is shiver."

Mehmet shrugged. "I don't have paper or pencils, much less books."

"You can clear a place where it's flat near the fire and write in the dirt," Mama said. "At least you can help them with their letters and numbers."

It wasn't much of a school, with Mehmet writing words in the dirt while a dozen shrill voices screamed out the sounds and a dozen small bodies jumped up and down to keep warm. He pretended to hate it, but it was plain to Meli that he relished being in charge. He was almost as proud of being "Teacher" as he was of the caterpillar fuzz that had sprouted from his upper lip about the time of his fourteenth birthday in October. He even borrowed a ball from the military camp and found an almost level spot lower on the hillside where the boys could play soccer. Naturally, girls were not allowed to join in, but Mehmet permitted them to watch and to chase the ball when it rolled downhill away from their playing field.

To Meli's surprise, children flocked to the makeshift school. They may have been shivering in the weak sunshine, but they still seemed to be listening to Mehmet. Even the smallest ones tried hard to write in the dirt the words he was teaching them.

"I teach only Albanian words," he said proudly. "When the revolution is won, there will be no need for Serbian obscenities."

Finally, one day Meli heard a rattling sound that really did turn into Uncle Fadil's Lada. A tired Baba and a weary Uncle Fadil climbed out. She ran and threw her arms around her father's neck. "Oh, Baba. I thought you were never coming back."

He patted her head as though she were Vlora's age. "Don't fret, little one," he said. "First we had to bring in the harvest. A farmer can't leave his fields at such a time, you know. And"—he paused and looked around to make sure his younger children were not in earshot—"Milosević has called back most of his army. It's safer to travel."

It didn't take long to pack, for they had far fewer goods than they had had when they arrived. Only Mehmet seemed reluctant to leave.

"I'm needed here," he told his father. "I—I run the school. All the children count on me."

"We need you too, my son," Baba said. "We can't risk losing you again."

"Next year I'll be fifteen," Mehmet muttered to Meli, but he climbed up over the front seat of the car and into the back to sit down between his brothers. He was grimly quiet the first several miles as they wound their way down the hill away from the encampment. "He still treats me like a child," he said to Meli over Isuf's head.

Meli couldn't say what she wanted to: *But you are a child.* It would only have made him angrier. So instead she said, "Baba knows best, Mehmet. You know he only wants what is best for each of us."

Mehmet gave his horse snort. How she hated that insolent noise! He used to worship their father, and now . . . But everything would be all right again, she told herself. Baba had come, and he and Uncle Fadil were in charge. They were taking the family away from the mountains. Baba knew the mountains were no place for a boy so obviously thirsting for Serbian blood.

But what had happened to her big brother—the person she had alternately adored and resented all her life? What would become of him, poisoned as he was by such bitterness?

SIX

At Uncle Fadil's

THE DOOR WAS ALREADY OPEN WHEN THE LADA PULLED UP in front of Uncle Fadil's house. Auntie Burbuqe was standing there, her arms wide open to welcome them. But it was, as Baba had predicted, a crowded house. Meli had never seen such a pile of shoes at a door before. Granny was there, of course, sitting next to the stove, her head wrapped in her traditional scarf, her shawl pulled tightly around her narrow shoulders, and wearing her Turkish-style *dhimmi* trousers that came clear to the ankles. Nexima came out of one of the back bedrooms. She had indeed come home, bringing her three-year-old son, Elez, and her twin babies. Hamza, her husband, was nowhere to be seen, and no one spoke of him—which could only mean, Meli thought, that he was in the KLA. She had come to realize on the mountain that if a man had been killed, he was mourned aloud, and if he had disappeared, people worried about him, but if he was with the KLA, no one even breathed his name.

Nexima gave her bed in Granny's room to Mama and Baba, and she brought her children into the small parlor. The four of them were to sleep with the five young Lleshis. The couch pulled out, so Nexima and her children slept there. Cushions were put on the floor for the Lleshi children. The small space was carpeted with bodies. Baba took one look and laughed. "I've seen orange slices with more room than this," he said. Everyone laughed with him. It felt so good to laugh, and, actually, they were less crowded than they had been in the tent. They were a lot warmer, too, and there were no rocks poking into their backs.

The next morning the household was stirring by the time the first rooster crowed. Uncle Fadil and Baba were like the generals of a little army. Everyone except Nexima's three had duties to carry out. The cow and the goats had to be milked and given hay, the chickens fed. Meli found herself in charge of the water brigade. Uncle Fadil didn't have running water in the farmhouse, but why should that bother her? A back-yard pump and a proper outhouse seemed luxurious after a mountain stream and a shack straddling it a short way down the hill.

Meli was so excited about her job as sergeant of the water detail that she had her little brothers and Vlora help her fill every pot she could lay her hands on. Auntie Burbuqe threw up her apron in mock amazement. "Ah," she said, "you children are such marvelous water carriers that you have left us nothing to cook in! Oh, well, fill up the tub—we'll have to bathe the babies before the day is done, I'm sure."

Uncle Fadil and Baba had brought in most of the crops while the family was waiting on the mountain, but there were still potatoes to be dug and wood to be chopped and split, and every day there were the chickens to be fed and the goats and cow to be milked.

Between his chores with the men, Mehmet held school for Isuf and Adil. Vlora was always jumping up and down, demanding to be included, so Mehmet soon gave up and let her join them. "But you have to be in charge of her," he said to Meli. It was the closest he came to suggesting that Meli, too, would be a teacher in *his* school. The house was too small for indoor classes, so the children put on their coats and once again held lessons outdoors. November in the plains felt much warmer than October in the hills.

Despite the crowding, Meli felt that she had never been happier. Even Mehmet seemed more content than he had since . . . well, since before the day of the pelican. Baba and Uncle Fadil took care to treat him as one of the men. The farm had the traditional men's chamber—a building behind the farmhouse that only men could enter—and when the brothers retreated to it, they often invited Mehmet to join them. Meli couldn't help but notice that when news from the outside world reached the farm, Mehmet was told first, even before Auntie Burbuqe or Mama.

So it was from Mehmet that Meli learned—even before they heard it on the radio—that the American ambassador was bringing in some cease-fire observers. "Observers!" Mehmet snorted at that. "They don't have any guns," he said. "What can they do? All they do is talk. They can yell and threaten all they like, but Milosević just thumbs his nose at them. We need action."

"But the threats worked," Meli argued. "Haven't most of the soldiers gone back to Serbia now?"

"Only a fool would trust that snake Milosević. Just wait. We'll be back at war in no time."

❄ ❄ ❄

Meanwhile, on the farm, peace reigned. The milking was done, the cheese made, the bread baked, the water pumped and brought in, the livestock as well as the large extended family fed. Auntie Burbuqe made the best pepper and eggplant sauce

Meli had ever tasted, but she was careful not to say this aloud. She wouldn't want to hurt Mama's feelings. They ate goat cheese with bread and pepper sauce, and thick potato soup. As a special treat, the women would make a savory cheese pie, which they filled with leeks or potatoes or spinach and even sometimes a bit of meat. The hunger of the lean days in the hills seemed long in the past.

The twins, with the nourishment of their mother's milk and constant attention from the rest of the family, were growing fatter and funnier by the day. While the others worked, they would often sit crammed together on Granny's lap, laughing while she tickled them and spoke to them in a language all their own. Meli was always eager for her turn with the twins. She couldn't remember enjoying her own little brothers and sister nearly so much. "Don't carry them all the time," Nexima half scolded her. "They'll never start walking."

Meli tried not to think of the continuing unrest in the country, but by January it could not be ignored. She secretly wondered how much of it was the KLA's fault. KLA soldiers had attacked four policemen near Racak, and the Serbian security forces retaliated by killing forty-five Albanians, then twenty-four more. NATO, that mysterious European military alliance led by the Americans, demanded that both sides meet in a peace conference in February. Milosević refused to attend. He sent, as Mehmet put it, "his flunkies" to represent Serbia, and by March, despite NATO's threats, Serbian troops were massing on the border of Kosovo.

"Didn't I tell you?" Mehmet said as they heard the news on Uncle Fadil's radio. "It'll be all-out war soon." He was smiling as he said this—with the kind of smile that made Meli's stomach knot. How could her brother smile at the thought of more killing and misery? But still, how else could Milosević be stopped?

❀ ❀ ❀

"They're going to do it!" Mehmet had come running from the house to where she was feeding the chickens.

"What? Who?"

"NATO is going to begin bombing the Serbs! Bill Clinton says so!" He was jubilant. "It was on television in America. They're really going to help us!"

How could Mehmet be so happy, Meli wondered. *Bombs don't know, when they fall, if you are a Serbian soldier or a Kosovar child. Bombs don't ask if you are guilty or innocent. They just fall, and if you are below, they kill you.*

The bombing began, so far away at first that it was only a dull thud in their ears. Then at night they heard the planes roaring overhead, and if they went outside they could both hear and see the distant explosions. Mehmet was beside himself with joy. Even Meli, for all her fears, couldn't suppress a thrill when she saw the sky light up.

But with the hoped-for NATO bombs came disaster. A westward parade began to pass by on the road below the farm: laden-down cars, overloaded wagons pulled by tractors, weary people on foot, all heading toward the Cursed Mountains—heading for Albania. Some stopped and asked for water or food. Some reported that they had been driven from their farms by masked men, others that a nearby village had been burned and they'd left rather than wait to be driven away—or killed. There had been killings, they said. Many killings. A woman to whom

Mama was giving water told her, "The man said, 'You wanted NATO? Ask NATO to help you now!' Then they killed my husband before my eyes and took me . . ." She saw Meli standing beside her mother and didn't finish the sentence.

❋ ❋ ❋

A few nights later, their time on the farm came to an abrupt end. Meli was sleeping close to the front door when she heard what seemed to be a gentle, rhythmic rapping.

She sat up and listened. Yes, someone was at the door. Should she open it? *Tap tap tap*—a pause—then *tap tap tap tap*. She was close by, but something held her back. She waited. There it was again: *tap tap tap*—pause—*tap tap tap tap*.

She must get Baba. He would know what to do. She slid out from under her blanket and made her way carefully across the sleeping bodies on the parlor floor toward Granny's room, but before she could get there, she met Uncle Fadil stumbling out of his own bedroom.

"I think," Meli whispered, "I think there's someone at the door."

He put his finger to his lips. "I'll handle it. Go back to sleep."

Meli followed him back across the hillocks of bodies, both taking care not to let their feet touch any of them. She stood for a moment in her place by the door, listening. *Tap tap tap*—pause—*tap tap tap tap*.

"Lie down," her uncle commanded. "Go back to sleep."

She lay down obediently, but how could she help but hear Uncle Fadil whisper through a crack in the door, "What is it? Why are you here? It's too dangerous—"

"I had to tell you—you must leave. At once."

Uncle Fadil slipped out the door and closed it silently be-hind him. Meli knew she was disobeying, but she couldn't help herself. She crept to the door and put her ear against it.

"How can I leave?" Uncle Fadil was saying. "This is the land of my father's fathers . . ."

"For God's sake," the voice was pleading, "they have no mercy. They've already destroyed the farms just north of here. I beg you. For the lives of my wife and children . . ."

So it was Hamza out there.

"Where would we go? How could we—with the bombing?"

"Go to Albania. Right away. There's not much time, I tell you."

"I must talk to Hashim. And there's Granny. How could she bear—"

"Please, please. Just go. Just leave here. At once . . . I have to go now. Leave at once, I beg you."

"I'll tell Nexima you were here."

"No, no, you can't. No one must know I came."

"God go with you, my son. May your life be lengthened."

There was a whispered response. "May your life be lengthened."

By the time Uncle Fadil slipped back into the house, Meli was wrapped in her blanket, pretending sleep, but her heart was pounding and her head reeling. There were too many of them—fourteen people, not counting clothing, bedding, and food. How could they all crowd into Uncle Fadil's Lada? Even if they took nothing with them for the journey . . . and how long a journey would it be and to where?

❊ ❊ ❊

The next day she went through the motions of living. She fetched the water and helped peel potatoes. She tried to eat the good food the women prepared, but she strained always to see if Uncle Fadil and Baba had talked and, if they had, what they had decided. Hamza had said they must leave at once, but she couldn't detect any signs of packing, any indication that this was anything more than an ordinary day.

It was midafternoon when Baba came out to where Mehmet and Meli were holding school. Mehmet was in the midst of his daily lecture on Kosovo's history—explaining once again why the Serbs had no right to "our land"—when Baba appeared. "Mehmet," he said, "come to the men's chamber, please." Meli's mouth went dry. Now it would happen—whatever it was. The men, with Mehmet, would go into the men's chamber and decide their fate. "Care for the children, Meli," Baba added. She nodded, too numb even to resent Mehmet's inclusion in a decision that might change their lives forever.

Not long afterward they were all called into the parlor. Baba cleared his throat. "We have decided that we must leave the farm as soon as possible."

There was a murmur among the women.

"Why do we have to leave?" Adil asked. "I like it here."

"We all love the farm, Adil," Baba said. "But, you know, with all the bombing and . . . and other things, it may not be safe for us to stay."

"Where are we going?" Isuf asked the question they were all longing to ask.

"We're going to Macedonia . . . for now," Uncle Fadil said. "Until it's safe to come home," he added.

"Yes," said Baba, "until then."

Macedonia! But Macedonia is a whole other country. I've never even been to Prishtina. Meli kept these thoughts to herself.

"How do we get to Macedonia?" Adil asked. For him the neighboring country must have seemed a world away. It almost did to Meli.

"We'll go in Uncle Fadil's car, of course," Baba said. "You remember how it took us to the mountains? Well, now it's going to take us all the way to Macedonia. It will be a new adventure for us all."

"Hmmph." It was hardly more than a grunt, but Meli gave Mehmet a jab with her elbow. As hard as it was to imagine all of them jamming into the Lada, he mustn't scare the little ones. Later she told him so.

"I won't say anything," he said. "But they're making a big mistake."

"What do you mean?" She hadn't told anyone, even Mehmet, that she'd heard Hamza's warning. "Don't we have to leave?"

"Oh, we have to leave all right. It's this crazy plan to go to Macedonia. Just because we have some cousin there. We should go to Albania."

That's what Hamza said. And yet . . . "Doesn't Baba know what's best for us?" she asked.

"Not always," he said, and walked away.

Since the car had to carry them all, there wasn't much they could take along. Each child and each adult would carry a blanket and wear two sets of clothing. The twins had to have more—babies needed diapers, after all. The women would take enough bread, cheese, and water to last a couple of days. And maybe a coil of sausage or two to share with the relatives.

That should be more than enough, since they would reach Macedonia in a few hours. The extra day of provisions was in case . . . well, just in case. The children watched sadly as Uncle Fadil opened the gates to the paddocks so the animals could go free. But the animals didn't leave. They just seemed confused, especially the cow, with her great brown eyes. *Why must I suffer because of human evil?* she seemed to be saying.

Meli dressed in her two sets of clothes. It was all she had owned since the family had left home the year before. The clothes were beginning to get tight, but her only sweater was a baggy one, and, fortunately, her jacket still fit.

The men spread most of the blankets in the back of the car and put in the food and water. Mama and Auntie Burbuqe took the cheese and bread, a soup pot, and some mugs and spoons for everyone. When Uncle Fadil hesitated, Auntie insisted. "They'll fit right in the pot, and I'll carry it on my lap. We can't expect the relatives to have enough for all of us." Meli saw Mama take out her beloved photograph, sigh, and then carefully put it back into Auntie Burbuqe's china cabinet.

"There's room for that, Mama," Meli said. "I'll take care of it."

Mama shook her head and smiled. "It's all right, Meli. We'll get it when we return."

At last they were ready. "Go lie down, everyone. Try to rest," Uncle Fadil said. "As soon as it is dark, we'll be on our way."

Meli was sure that she wouldn't be able to sleep. She lay down on the cushioned floor and tried to quiet her noisy mind, but old television images of the devastation in Bosnia crowded in. Was Kosovo just another Bosnia, then? Were they all helpless against Milosević and his armies? Would they just be fleeing the tyrant all their lives, never, ever going home?

Somehow, despite all, she must have dozed off, because the next thing she heard was Mehmet shouting from outside the door.

"It's gone! The car! Someone's stolen the car!"

SEVEN

Road to the Unknown

FOR A LONG WHILE THEY ALL JUST GAPED AT THE EMPTY space where the Lada should have been. How could they believe that it was gone? It was like a sudden death in the family, totally incomprehensible.

"I didn't hear it start," said Uncle Fadil. "There was no noise."

"It was a very noisy car," said Isuf.

"It was the noisiest old car in the whole world," said Adil.

"They must have pushed it down the road before they tried to start it," Baba said.

"A long way," said Isuf.

Adil was nodding his head solemnly. "A really long way."

Another time they would have all laughed, but not tonight. Meli could hear Mehmet cursing the Serbs under his breath, but of course there was no way of knowing who had stolen the Lada.

"To come in the night and steal our car and everything in it!" Auntie Burbuqe wailed.

"The wolf loves the fog," Mama said sadly.

"I should never have bought a car. I should have gotten a bigger tractor," Uncle Fadil said, burying his face in his hands. "I should have listened to you, Hashim. They wouldn't have stolen a tractor."

"Ah, they would have stolen anything." Baba put his hand on his brother's shoulder. "Don't blame yourself." Then, wiping his face with his big white handkerchief, he said almost to himself, "Well, wishing won't bring it back." He put the hand-kerchief into his pocket, took another long look at the empty parking spot, and turned toward the house. "We'll hitch the tractor to the wagon and go in that. Sevdie, Burbuqe, surely there's plenty more food in the kitchen."

"Nexima," Uncle Fadil said, "you'd better get Granny dressed. We need to be ready . . ."

For anything, thought Meli. But how did you prepare for that?

As the men set to work hitching up the wagon and loading more bread and cheese and sausage, the women began silently to clean an already spotless kitchen. They could hear the men talking as they worked. What were the men saying? What plan could save them now?

"We should just stay here," Auntie Burbuqe declared, break-ing the silence. "Take our chances here. That tractor isn't very powerful, and the wagon is much too small for all of us."

Mama shook her head. "I don't know," she said. "I just don't know. Let's wait and hear what they think. They must have some ideas." *She's remembering that woman,* thought Meli, *the one with the terrible story.* Occasionally, they could hear Mehmet's voice, raised in argument. *It's already past dawn. How much longer are they going to keep talking and arguing out there?*

At last they came in. "We should eat something before we start," Baba said. "It is a long way, and we'll have to take turns walking."

Auntie Burbuqe and Mama dished out some leftover soup. They didn't want to take the time to make a fire, so they ate it cold, along with a bit of bread and sausage. No one had much appetite.

"Fetch some more water for the trip, Meli," said Mama. "What you drew earlier . . ."

Meli got a bucket from the kitchen and ran out to the well, grateful for something to do. Then, over the creak of the pump, she heard a sound—the sound of a motor. Her hand stopped in midair. She squeezed her eyes closed and willed it to be the well-known noisy clunking of Uncle Fadil's old Lada, coming home like a lost dog to its owner. But it was no use pretending. What she was listening to was the unfamiliar sound of a newer, smoother-running car. Grabbing the half-filled pail, Meli ran for the kitchen door.

"Someone's coming!"

At first everyone was frozen in place, listening. As the sound grew louder, they began to gravitate toward the living room, as if drawn there by some outside force. No one spoke. Louder and louder the motor sounded; then they heard the squeal of brakes. Meli held her breath, counting as car doors slammed—one, two, three, four—and then, without warning, the front door flew open. Five men in ski masks burst into the room. Four of the men held rifles at the ready; the fifth was waving a huge pistol. These were new weapons, not the old castoffs carried by the KLA. One of the intruders went into Uncle Fadil's bedroom and came back carrying a pillowcase. The man with the pistol pointed at Mama and Auntie Burbuqe and Nexima. "Take off all that gold," he ordered. "Rings, necklace, bracelets—everything."

As the women struggled to pull their rings off fingers that had grown thicker with the years, he got more and more impatient. "Faster, or I'll have to cut them off."

Another of the men made Baba and Uncle Fadil empty their pockets—money, licenses, ID cards of any sort. "So we won't be able to prove we live here," Mehmet muttered.

"Quiet!" one of the men ordered.

When all the valuables had been put into the pillowcase, the pistol wielder yelled, "Get out now! All of you—out! This house belongs to the Serbian people. Why are you standing there like fools? I said get out!"

Just then Granny appeared at the kitchen door. She was dressed, as usual, in her baggy *dhimmi* trousers, a large overshirt, and an old stretched sweater, with her headscarf tied over what was left of her thin white hair. She was hugging the shawl that hung around her shoulders. For a few seconds she stared at the intruders, squinting her watery eyes. "Who are these people?" she asked querulously.

One of the masked men stepped forward and poked her with the end of his long rifle. "Give me your gold!"

Granny just stared at him.

"She's a widow. She has no gold," Baba said.

"Then get out, old woman!" the man shouted, poking her again with his gun.

"Show some respect," Baba said quietly. "She doesn't—"

The gunman turned his barrel toward Baba. "Shut up and get out before we lose patience with the lot of you."

"I don't want to go out," said Granny, holding her shawl tightly to her waist. "Why do I have to go out?" She looked more confused than Nexima's three-year-old.

"Come, Mama," Baba said gently, taking her arm. "It's time to leave."

One of the babies began to cry. "Get that brat out of here, or I will shut it up." The one with the pistol took aim at the baby's head.

They hurried out then, grabbing up shoes, jostling one another through the narrow doorway, but once in the yard they hesitated. Where were they to go?

"And leave that tractor and wagon right where they are. They belong to us!" one of the men shouted from the open door.

"We'll need it to take our livestock!" another taunted.

"And anything worth the bother," said a third.

"Get the wheelbarrow, Mehmet," Baba said under his breath. "And fast." There was no need to add "fast." Mehmet was gone and back almost before Baba had finished the sentence.

Baba picked Granny up and put her carefully into the wheelbarrow. Her legs dangled over the edge, and her *dhimmi* were hiked up halfway to her knees. Baba tried to pull the trouser legs down, but he couldn't tug them as far as her ankles. She was still clutching at her waist. *She must be so embarrassed.* Meli found herself blushing for the old woman. Granny had always been so traditional, wearing a headscarf and *dhimmi*. But as immodest and as uncomfortable as she looked, Meli saw that Granny was smiling at Baba as though she were Vlora being given a ride for a treat.

"Let's go," Baba said, lifting the handles. "Everyone. As quickly as you can."

They half ran the first few yards but soon slowed to a walk. How could they run? Auntie and Nexima each carried a twin, Uncle Fadil was carrying the three-year-old Elez, and Mama was holding Vlora's hand, trying to urge her along. Meli didn't dare look over her shoulder. Suppose the masked men were chasing them? The horror that they might all be shot in the back made her turn, and when she did, she gasped aloud. Flames were leaping up to the early morning sky.

"Look!" she cried.

"The farm! They're burning our farm!" Uncle Fadil put his grandson on the ground and started to run toward the fire.

"Fadil!" Baba lowered the wheelbarrow and chased him down. He held tightly to his brother's arm. "You can't, brother. They'll kill you."

Uncle Fadil drooped like a dying plant. The brothers took one more look, then turned and came back to where the family was waiting. Huge tears were rolling down Uncle Fadil's sun-reddened face and catching in his mustache. The children stared at him. They couldn't help it; they had never seen a grown man cry before. Meli wanted to weep for him. *Baba didn't even cry when Mehmet was missing.*

"So." Uncle Fadil sniffed and wiped his face with the back of his big hand. "So. There's nothing to be done, is there? We must reconcile ourselves to it."

Meli could see that he was ashamed to be caught crying in front of them all. He picked up Elez and handed him to Baba, took the handles of the wheelbarrow, and began to push. Meli saw Granny twist around and kiss his arm, as though Uncle Fadil were still her little boy who needed comforting for a skinned knee.

❊ ❊ ❊

Heading east, they were making their way against a tide of refugees heading west toward Albania. *Maybe Mehmet was right. Maybe we are going in the wrong direction.* But they went grimly on. Meli wiped her forehead with her sleeve. It was miserable walking in her layers of clothing, her wool sweater and her jacket. For the first several hours, the only stops they made were hasty ones to exchange burdens. As they passed neighboring farms, they could see other cars like the one that had come to the farm, and other masked men loading them up with the contents of the houses. Some of the houses they passed had apparently been emptied and now were burning.

"So there'll be no place to come home to when this is over," muttered Mehmet.

Once they spied an outhouse with no one nearby, and they hastily took advantage of it. The road was growing more and more crowded with Albanian Kosovars fleeing their homeland, but the Lleshis seemed to be the only people going toward the center of the country rather than away from it.

Everyone who was able took turns carrying the four small ones and pushing the wheelbarrow. Isuf and Adil, who seemed about to drop in their tracks, shook their heads manfully whenever Meli or Mehmet offered a piggyback ride. They stopped once for Nexima to feed the twins, but they were all too anxious to lie down, because the night sky was filled with the roar of planes overhead. Every time they heard the crash of bombs and saw the brilliant light of explosions, Mehmet gave a little cheer. "Hurray for Bill Clinton," he would say, not quite loudly enough for Baba to hear. Meli, standing beside him, was shaking at the sight of orange flames licking the dark sky. How could he be happy? People were losing their homes, perhaps dying in those flames.

It was nearly dawn when Isuf asked: "How much longer, Baba?"

"Not much longer, son. We must all be very brave and strong."

How, then, could Meli complain that she was tired? Little Adil wasn't even whining.

With the first streaks of light to the east, one of the babies began to cry. "We have to stop, Baba," Nexima said. "I must feed the babies again."

"We all need to rest," Auntie Burbuqe said.

The grass was wet with dew, but everyone sat down anyway. There was no use thinking about food for anyone but the babies. Meli tried to remind herself that she had had a good meal just the evening before—sausage, bread, cheese, yogurt—and there had been that sort of breakfast earlier in the day of cold soup . . . She stopped herself. Her mouth was parched. There wasn't even any water to drink, not even a pot to draw water in. She thought of all the pots and pails she had filled with cool well water at Uncle Fadil's house.

Nexima finished nursing the twins. They should move on. They had to hurry. *Suppose some Serb militants find us here, just sitting on the grass? They'll kill us all,* Meli thought, but she was too tired to stand up.

"There's a farm a bit farther down this road," Uncle Fadil was saying, "where I know the farmer. He's a good man. He'll let us have some water. He might even offer us something to eat. Besides, he owes me a favor. I loaned him my billy goat last year."

"If he still has a farm, he must be Serb," Mehmet said.

"Yes, but—"

"He won't remember he owes you anything," Mehmet said.

"He's a good man, I say."

"A good Serb," Mehmet said sarcastically. Baba gave Mehmet his *be quiet* look.

Uncle Fadil stood up. They watched him as he walked ahead to the old stone farmhouse, barely visible now in the distance. Reluctantly, the rest of the family got up and began to walk in the same direction. Meli held her breath as Uncle Fadil knocked on the door. In a minute or two the door opened a crack, then closed again.

"I told you," Mehmet muttered.

But Uncle Fadil didn't move. A few more minutes passed, and the door opened again. This time a little wider, and they could see a hand, holding out a pot. Uncle Fadil took the pot, nodded, and said something they couldn't hear. The door closed once more.

"Meli," Uncle Fadil called out as he came quickly back to them, "take this to the well in back." As tired as she was, she ran to obey. The pot was old and battered, but it held water. She pumped until it was filled to the brim. It was so heavy the narrow metal handle cut into her palm, but she carried it carefully, unwilling to lose a precious drop, and walked back to where the family waited.

"She said we could keep the pot," Uncle Fadil said, proud as a child who's won a school prize.

Not even Mehmet complained aloud that no food had been offered, or that the pot was so dented and stained Mama would have thrown it out long ago. It held water. That was what mattered. It would even boil soup, if they ever got the makings of soup and the means to start a fire.

When everyone had taken a good long drink, Meli returned to the well and filled the pot once more before they began to walk again. The water helped a bit to fill their empty stomachs, and it was not until they stopped to rest a couple of hours later that Meli was conscious of her stomach growling and churning. She had been far more aware of the metal pot handle cutting into her palm.

Nexima nursed the twins and then called her three-year-old and fed him as well.

Adil sidled over to where Meli was sitting. He put his thin little arm around her neck. "I'm hungry," he whispered in her ear.

"I know," she said. "We all are. When we come to a place where we can buy food, Baba will get us something." She remembered midsentence that their father's money was now in that pillowcase.

"When?"

She rubbed her brother's bony back. "Soon," she said. "Soon, I'm sure. We have to be very patient and very brave."

But even if there had been money, there were no shops selling bread in the villages they walked through. There were houses being looted as their owners fled, and every business seemed to have been burned or vandalized beyond repair. The road was filled with people just as hungry and desperate as they were. By midmorning they were too tired and hungry to walk another step. They knew they must keep walking, but as much as their minds told them to go on, their bodies simply refused to move.

"Hashim, Fadil," Mama said after they had passed through yet another burned village, "why don't we sleep now, while the grass is dry and the sun is warm? We can walk in the evening when it is too cool to sleep." The older children didn't wait for permission. They plopped down on the grass. Baba and Uncle Fadil put Vlora and Elez beside their mothers and then helped Granny out of the wheelbarrow. She groaned a bit when they set her on her feet. *Poor Granny*, thought Meli. *How stiff she must be, riding all those hours in that funny position over this bumpy road.*

The old woman straightened as much as her old back would let her and then looked around at all of them sprawled on the grass. "Are we having a picnic?" she asked. Mehmet gave a short laugh and got a look from Baba.

"No, Mother—" Uncle Fadil began, but stopped when they saw Granny reaching about under her shawl and overshirt and into the waist of her trousers. Auntie Burbuqe jumped up to keep her mother-in-law from pulling her clothes apart in front of them all. "Granny," she said, "what are you doing? Let me help you."

Just then Granny succeeded in pulling two loaves of bread out from under her voluminous overshirt.

"I was going to take them to the chickens," she said. "Then those bad men came. I didn't have time, so I . . ." She made a motion of sticking the bread into her waistband. She looked apologetic. "It's not so much for all these people."

"It's a feast!" Baba said. "You clever woman!"

Adil was on his feet, clapping his hands. "Clever Granny. You fooled the bad men!"

Granny smiled shyly as Uncle Fadil broke off pieces of the loaves and gave some to everyone. Even the babies had a piece to suck on. *Only someone who has ever really been hungry would understand how delicious this dry bread tastes*, thought Meli. They each ate their share, had a long drink of water, and, almost satisfied, lay down to sleep on the grass. Baba and Uncle Fadil agreed to take turns being on watch. When Meli woke up she saw that Mehmet was still sitting up, as wide-awake as he had been when she fell asleep.

❋ ❋ ❋

They began walking again that afternoon, and just as the night before, they were walking toward an endless procession of their countrymen heading westward. Though they weren't just walking now; they were climbing. Meli knew from all Mr. Uka's geography lessons that they must cross the hills into eastern Kosovo before they could reach Macedonia. Baba and Uncle Fadil were right, no matter what Mehmet thought. Surely the passes through the Cursed Mountains to the west and the Sharr range to the southwest would have been too much of a barrier for a family like theirs.

But although the distance seemed relatively short if you looked at a map, and the hills far gentler than the mountains, the walk from the Plain of Dukagjin to the eastern plain was a hard trek for the Lleshis. Cars and tractors pulling wagons loaded with people and household goods rolled slowly past them. Meli tried not to envy the riders or worry that she and her family were indeed heading in the wrong direction. She kept telling herself that they were all together. That was the important thing. They had one another. And a pot. A pot that held water. She guarded that old pot as carefully as if it had been Mama's treasured photo.

Once across the hills, they found that they were no longer walking against the flow of refugees. "Where are all these people coming from?" Meli asked Mehmet.

"Prishtina," he said.

It should have been easier, walking with the crowd instead of against it, but if they stumbled in their weariness, they found themselves pushed and jostled from behind. Once Meli caught Baba counting heads, making sure everyone was still there, still together in the crowd. Around them there was a constant clamor of conversation, of children crying and adults trying to comfort or cajole. On and on they walked. Then, without warning, the clamor turned to shrieks.

"Get off the road!" someone screamed, and as soon as they did, three cars came racing into their midst. Almost before the vehicles came to a stop, Serb policemen were jumping out of the doors, shouting at the crowd, "This way! This way!"

"Hold on to the boys, Meli," Baba ordered. "Don't let them separate us."

In her haste, she dropped the precious pot. It rolled away, clanging on rocks. Should she try to get it? No, she must hold on to her brothers. The pot was gone. She grabbed Isuf's and Adil's hands and pressed as close to Baba and Granny's wheelbarrow as she could.

"This way! This way!" the policemen kept yelling, herding the Albanians as though they were balky sheep, pushing them across railroad tracks and down toward a tiny rail station. One of the policemen grabbed the handles of Granny's wheelbarrow. He started to tip it up as though he was going to dump her out. Mehmet jumped forward to catch her.

"Get her out of my way!" the man ordered.

Carefully, Mehmet helped Granny to her feet. She swayed and clutched at Mehmet.

The policeman waved his pistol in the air. "Hurry!"

"My grandmother has trouble walking," Mehmet said, glowering at the policeman.

"Not another word," Baba muttered. He lifted Granny in his arms and began to walk, all the family close behind.

EIGHT

Terror and Tragedy

To MELI IT FELT AS THOUGH THEY WERE WAITING FOR A train that was never coming. Eventually, people began to sit down on the platform. She tried not to think about the stories she'd read in school about trains that took people to concentration camps and death. She tried not to watch the policemen, who were patrolling the edges of the crowd, waving their guns in the air, threatening to shoot troublemakers. There was to be no food, no water, even. And, more immediately, she was desperate to relieve herself. She whispered this to Mama.

Finally, Baba got up and went over to speak to one of the policemen. The man nodded angrily. Baba came back and spoke softly to Mama. He had gotten permission for them to use the toilets in the station. Meli got up gratefully, taking Vlora by the hand. She hesitated, looking at Baba and Mehmet and her little brothers. She was afraid to let them out of her sight even for a minute, but she really couldn't wait any longer.

Mama was half carrying Granny. Auntie Burbuqe and Nexima each carried a twin, so Meli took little Elez's hand. With a hundred pardons and excuses, they made their way through the crowd to the toilets. Meli was terrified that once others saw where they were headed, the room would be mobbed and they'd never get in, but they got there first, before the crowd realized what was happening. They were wearing so much clothing, it was a struggle to use the toilet. She helped Vlora first, then went herself. By the time they were at the basins, trying to clean up a bit, women and children were pouring into the small room. Meli quickly washed Vlora's and Elez's faces with her hand and splashed cool water on her own filthy face and hands before they had to squeeze out to leave space for others as needy as themselves.

It was well after midnight when they heard the long whistle of an oncoming train. Meli's relief turned to horror when she saw that the engine coming to a halt was pulling a long line of freight cars. It was just like the terrifying old stories. Policemen flung open the huge sliding doors. The metallic rattle echoed down the line like the death throes of a mechanical beast.

"Hold on to each other!" Baba's voice pierced her fear. "Tight! Hold on tight!"

"Move! Move! You lazy pigs! Get up there! Now!" The police used their big pistols to push and shove the Albanians up and into the cars. With babies crying and old people whimpering and the frightened crowd pushing and shoving, Meli was terrified that she would let go of Adil's and Isuf's small hands, but she clung to them as though all their lives depended on it. Baba and Uncle Fadil helped Mama, Auntie Burbuqe, and Nexima up first. Then they handed Granny and Nexima's children and Vlora up to them before they climbed in themselves.

"Meli, Mehmet," Baba called. "Help the boys!" Meli hesitated. How could she hand one brother up without letting go of the other's hand?

"I've got him," Mehmet said, and he slung Isuf up to Baba's waiting arms as though he were nothing but a small parcel. Then it was Adil's turn.

"Now you, Meli," Mehmet said.

Again she hesitated. She was nearly as heavy as Mehmet. "Come on!" he barked, grabbing her around the waist and hoisting her up so that she was on her knees, falling forward into the crowded interior. Baba pulled her to her feet and then, holding to the side of the car, leaned out and pulled Mehmet to safety. Seconds later a policeman came by and gave the door a powerful shove, and they were plunged into darkness.

She heard Baba and Uncle Fadil calling everyone's name. No one was missing. They might die, but they would at least die together.

There was no room for most people to sit down, although Meli learned later that Baba and Uncle Fadil had managed to get Granny to the side of the car, where she could sit leaning against the metal wall. Meli herself could only stand in the crowded boxcar, sweating in her two dresses, her sweater, and her jacket. She held on to her little brothers by their hands, their shoulders, their jacket collars—anything to keep contact with them in the dark.

She would never know just how long the family was on the train. It simply sat at the station for what seemed like hours before it began noisily to move, waking up all the sleeping children. Then it went for what could hardly have been more than a few yards before it squealed and shuddered to a stop. This happened over and over again, each time the train stopping so suddenly that it would throw the occupants hard against each other. Once Meli heard Adil cry out in alarm. *Don't let him be crushed*, she prayed.

She tried not to think of the smell. At first it was simply the sweat and dirt of the journey, but as the night wore on it became the unmistakable smell of human waste and vomit. If there was such a thing as hell, it could not be worse than this.

And then, although it seemed to Meli that an eternity had passed with the train hardly moving, the doors flew open. Unaccustomed to the light, she stood still, blinking for several moments before she realized that it was morning.

"Out! Out!" On the ground were soldiers in Serbian uniforms.

"Stay together!" As loud as the crowd was, she could still hear Baba's command. "Hold on to each other!"

"Out!"

Staying as close to each other as possible, the family came down from the boxcar. Meli could feel the point of a rifle between her shoulder blades as she held up her arms to take Adil from Mehmet. There was so much noise and confusion that she just focused on grabbing her little brothers by their jackets. Baba was carrying Granny. Meli pushed through the crowd toward him. She hoped they didn't have far to go now that they were without their wheelbarrow.

Everyone from the train was being herded in the same direction. "Go on! Hurry! Get out!" the soldiers were shouting.

Get out of where? What did they mean? And then she realized that they meant *Get out of Kosovo*. They were being thrown out of their homeland—like garbage. *We are people!* Meli longed to yell. *Not pigs or trash. I used to have good clothes and live in a nice apartment. I used to read books and watch TV and go to films. I used to comb my hair and brush my teeth and misbehave in school.* But of course she said nothing. No one did. They didn't want to tempt some angry soldier to use his gun.

Just then Meli heard a shout. "Nexima!"

She looked up. From a boxcar far up the line, pushing his way through the crowd, was Hamza. "Here," said Nexima, holding out to Meli the twin she was carrying.

"No," Meli cried, "you mustn't." *We have to stay together.* It was all she could think of. She dropped Isuf's hand and grabbed Nexima's arm. People closed in around them.

A single shot cracked the air. Nexima's head jerked back as though she herself had been hit. She would have fallen, baby and all, except that Meli was holding her so tightly. For a few seconds there was a stunned silence.

Meli could see nothing over the heads of the crowd, so they would never know if it was that shot that took Nexima's husband from his family. Nor would Meli ever know if she had done the right thing. Baba had said they must all stay together. She could not let Nexima go.

❈ ❈ ❈

It had been almost a year since they had left their comfortable life behind—two days since they'd left Uncle Fadil's happy, crowded farmhouse that was no more. They might never see Hamza again, but the rest of the family was still together. Mehmet had not disappeared into the KLA—or worse. Baba and Uncle Fadil were still in charge. Granny had survived the terrible journey, and even though her mind was more like a child's than Vlora's was, it was she who had smuggled bread right past those hoodlums. Remembering it, Meli almost smiled.

The surging crowd stopped so suddenly that she fell against the woman in front of her. What was happening? As usual, it was Mehmet who seemed to know. "The Macedonian border guards won't let anyone cross. There are too many of us."

Meli's heart sank. They couldn't go backward; they would be shot. And now they couldn't go forward.

NINE

The Bus

HOLD ON TO EACH OTHER," BABA SAID, JUST AS HE'D BEEN saying for hours. "Follow me." Somehow they all edged themselves out of the center of the crowd that had just been forced off the train, and they made their way toward a patch of brown grass. Meli felt close to collapse, but there was no hope of rest. The Serbs behind them were screaming at them to go forward. Where were they to go?

"No man's land," muttered Mehmet. "They've dumped us into no man's land."

"Come on," said Baba, looking up at the sun to get his bearings. "We have to go south."

Everyone seemed to know the direction at the same time, and again they were being jostled and pushed by the crowd. Meli had thought they couldn't stand on their feet another minute, but how could she complain? Baba and Uncle Fadil were taking turns carrying Granny, and the women were carrying Elez and the twins. She stumbled forward, holding Adil's and Isuf's hands, while Mehmet carried Vlora piggyback. She glanced over her shoulder. The Serbian soldiers were making no attempt to follow. They seemed to be checking that the train was empty and pushing those who lagged behind in the direction of those who were walking. She thought she heard more shots, but she tried to block out the sounds. They'd been on their feet all night, nearly suffocating in the crowded boxcar. She was too tired for terror and too filthy to think of much else. Still, when they had walked until they could see in the distance another line of soldiers, she could feel the sudden racing of her heart.

"What is that?" she asked Mehmet.

"Macedonians," he answered. "They don't want us, either."

Once again Baba maneuvered the family to the edge of the mass of refugees. He set Granny gently on the ground. "Sit down," he said. "We all have to rest. You, too, Mehmet." Mehmet was standing, grim-faced, his arms tightly crossed. Baba touched his son's shoulder lightly. "It's all right," he said.

"Unless these bastards decide to kill us," Mehmet muttered as he sat down beside Meli. She had thought she was past feeling anything, but it still hurt to hear Mehmet sound so disrespectful to Baba. He mustn't lose faith in their father. Where would they be without him? Baba was their rock.

As exhausted as she was, she couldn't close her eyes. She listened to the cries of the crowd as they tried to push their way through the border crossing into Macedonia, and to the shouts of the soldiers determined to keep them out. She also heard through all that pandemonium the whimpering of hungry children and, quite near, just behind her, in fact, Granny coughing until she was almost choking. She could not bear to turn around and look.

What will become of us? Meli was too tired to cry, although the unspent tears pressed down like a giant weight on her heart.

❊ ❊ ❊

It seemed like days, but it must have been only three or four hours—the sun was still high in the south—when she heard the sound of a large vehicle, then several. Buses were coming through the border gate.

"Quickly now," Baba said, jumping to his feet. "We must all get on the same bus. Hold on to each other. Don't get separated."

Mehmet had already picked up Adil. Meli grabbed Isuf's hand. Mama carried Vlora, and Baba had Granny. Uncle Fadil, Auntie Burbuqe, and Nexima each carried a child. The crowd had parted to let the buses through, and, miraculously, when the buses stopped, the family was almost next to an open door. They climbed in and fell into seats near the front. Baba craned his head around and counted to make sure everyone was there.

"Where are we going?" Isuf asked.

"I don't know," Meli answered, and for once she hardly cared. They were going. They were leaving the horror behind. She could hear sobbing from a seat a few rows back. Meli turned and saw an old woman. She was being held by a younger woman, who was trying to soothe her.

"My husband. Oh, my husband," the old woman was crying. "Why do they shoot him? He do nothing. Nothing."

Meli couldn't make herself look across at Nexima. She couldn't bear to. She could only hope her cousin hadn't heard.

When the bus was full, with people cramming the narrow aisle, the driver slammed the door shut, backed up, and jerked forward.

"Where are you taking us?" someone asked.

"Don't take us back!" another voice yelled.

Someone started up the aisle. "They'll kill us all. You must not—"

"Sit down and shut up," the driver said. "You're going to a camp like the rest of them."

A camp. First the boxcar, now a camp. Through bleary eyes Meli stared at her family. They were hungry, filthy, exhausted—and homeless. No home to go back to and none to look forward to. And what was Nexima thinking now? *Oh, my husband! Why do they shoot him?* There in that crowded bus she saw not only those she loved but strangers—people she had never met—who were now one with them in loss and suffering and death. Something was tearing at the numbness inside her. It was ripping the lid off a feeling she had tried for months not to acknowledge. And what was that? Nothing less than the one evil of the human heart that Baba had always feared and abhorred. She knew now that hatred lurked there, just below the surface, and that if it escaped, it might consume her.

❀ ❀ ❀

By the time the bus finally pulled to a stop, it was clear that Granny was burning with fever. They all got off the bus as ordered and stood together in line, waiting to be told what to do. Baba and Uncle Fadil took turns holding Granny in their arms. They didn't want to put her down on the cold ground.

As the family neared the front of the line, Meli heard words spoken in some foreign tongue and then another voice speaking in Albanian. She peered around Uncle Fadil to see who was talking to Baba. The first speaker was a light-haired foreigner, one of several sitting at a long table; beside her was someone who seemed to be an Albanian man, interpreting for her. First the woman spoke and then the man said, "Take your mother to the hospital tent. Wilfried, that man over there, will show you the way." Baba, with only a quick glimpse back at the family, followed the young man. He had to go, of course—he had to get Granny help—but still . . . They watched him until he was out of sight.

"Your family will be in tent 147 B." The interpreter hesitated, looking at the remaining twelve Lleshis gathered before her, still standing close together and holding on to one another. She said something to the man. "Is this just one family?" he asked.

"Yes," said Uncle Fadil. "One family."

"Two," said Mama. They all looked at her in amazement.

"I mean," said Mama, reddening under the family's gaze, "there are too many for one small tent."

When this was translated, the woman seemed to agree, checking a list. "She says she can't put you side by side. The only other available large tent is in A—172 A." She looked at Mama and said something else. "She says, 'Do you have any blankets?'"

Mama looked at Uncle Fadil. She'd said too much already.

"No," he said.

"Not even a stove for cooking?"

He shook his head. "Everything was stolen."

There was another exchange.

"She says, 'As soon as you get something to eat . . .'"

"Eat?" Adil came suddenly to life.

The woman smiled at him just as though she understood, and the man said, "After you eat, go to the supply tent. They will give you blankets."

"Where do we go for food?" Uncle Fadil asked. "The children have had almost nothing for two days."

The man stood up and pointed. "You see that big tent over there? That's the meal tent. They'll begin serving"—he looked at his watch—"in about an hour. In the meantime, you can wash up—at that table over there you can get your water ration—and get settled in your tents."

Mama hesitated. "My husband," she began, looking out at the ocean of tents, "how will he find us if we leave this place?"

The interpreter spoke to the woman who beckoned with her right hand to a spot behind the long table. "She says to wait here until he gets back."

"Meli," Mehmet said, "let's go find the tents. Then we can take everyone straight there as soon as Baba gets back." She liked Mehmet wanting her to help him. It didn't usually happen unless Mama or Baba suggested it. Mama was glad, too. She smiled and nodded, and they were off to the rows of small, drab tents, searching for the numbers they'd been given. Children were running about everywhere, but most of the adults were just sitting on the ground in front of their tents as though waiting for something.

Mehmet went inside 147 B. "Well," he said when he came out, "it's no palace, but it's larger than the one on the mountain. Anyhow, we won't be here long. Milosević and his dirty Serbs can't beat Bill Clinton and NATO."

At the sound of the Serbian president's name, Meli could feel that ripped lid scraping open again. She put her hand to her chest to quiet it.

"Yes," Mehmet was saying, "trust me, we'll be home before summer."

He sounded so sure, but how could he know what would happen? The only sure thing they'd known for a long time was turmoil.

TEN

Refugees

LIVING IN THE REFUGEE CAMP WAS, AS MEHMET PUT IT, LIKE being chickens sentenced to jail. Meli tried to laugh at the idea, but they were indeed living behind a tall chicken-wire fence topped by barbed wire. There were armed guards at the single gate to keep people from coming in, and, of course, from going out. *Though where would we go?* And were they being protected from the Macedonians or were the Macedonians being protected from them? Still, life in camp was a welcome relief from the days of terror and exhaustion that they'd gone through. There was water: it came in a large plastic bag with a spigot at the bottom, and they hung it on a pole outside the tent. She heard someone say that it had too much chlorine in it, but it was clean and, if they were careful, enough for the day's needs. The food was plain, but they never went hungry. There were cold showers at least once a week and privies that smelled but hardly ever overflowed. Perhaps it was harder for Uncle Fadil's family, who had never camped out in the hills, but no one complained. They felt safe in this tent city. They were together.

Meli sensed a deep sadness in her cousin Nexima, but Hamza's name was never mentioned among them. It was as though he were still alive in the mountains with the KLA. And maybe he was. Maybe the shot they heard had not taken Hamza's life. She hoped so, even though there was little basis for hope.

The young international volunteers were cheerful and tried to make life bearable. To Mehmet's regret there was no space for a soccer field in their area of the huge camp, but one of the volunteers strung up a net and provided a ball, so the men and boys played endless games of volleyball. Anything, Mehmet said, was better than the boredom of just sitting around doing nothing.

The girls and women had no such diversion. Sometimes Meli watched the games. No, not the games themselves, but the players. The men and older boys attacked the ball with fury, as though with every hit they were taking revenge on all the losses they had endured. Even men who were quiet by nature, like Baba and Uncle Fadil, now yelled with every point scored and shouted encouragement to their teammates whenever a point was lost.

She would watch them, almost trembling in her fear for them, thinking, *What if they lose the game?*—completely forgetting it was just that, a game in a refugee camp, not the life-and-death struggle of the past year.

Mehmet was the worst. Though he was shorter than most of the men, he made up for it with his wild play, jumping into the air with a scream to smash the ball into the face of an opponent. Even if the others cried out that he should pass the ball, he never did. He always wanted to slam it across with all his might. And yet, as she watched, there was something in her that did understand his ferocious play. How she would have loved to give that ball the name of her enemies and smack it to the earth. She was becoming just like Mehmet, she thought. Although for Baba's sake she didn't express her hatred, she could no longer hide it from herself.

Whenever she became too overwrought watching the endless games, she'd wander back to the tent. Mama busied herself cleaning the tiny enclosure, but it was impossible to keep dust and dirt out of things. She made sure everyone left their shoes outside the tent—after all, it was their home, and no one would wear shoes in their home. They obeyed, just as they had at the camp in the hills, though it seemed a little crazy. There was so little difference between indoors and outdoors in a camp. Often Meli would find that Mama and the younger children had gone to Uncle Fadil's tent. There Vlora and the boys would play made-up games with Elez and the twins. Meli would watch them chasing each other about, screaming with delight, and wish that she weren't too old to join in their silly play. She would be thirteen on June 15. She wasn't interested in the women's chatter, she couldn't join the all-male volleyball, and she was past racing about with the young ones. Some days she thought about the rough KLA camp and missed it. There had been so much to do there—gathering wood, making fires, cooking.

"I think I'll go over to the hospital tent and see Granny," she would say, and Mama and Auntie Burbuqe would nod approvingly.

"Tell her we'll be over soon," they'd say. "And take her out for a little walk. She mustn't lie in bed all day."

The hospital tent was crowded with cots, but it was better for Granny, with her weak old body, than sleeping on the ground.

Meli would sit on the edge of the cot and try to make conversation, but Granny was usually confused. She often thought she was in Uncle Fadil's house and that someone had put her in the wrong bed. Then she would look around, puzzled. "Why are all these people in my house?" she'd ask.

Meli got in the habit of saying as soon as she sat down, "Hello, Granny; it's me, Meli. I've come to take you out into the sunshine. It's a lovely day." She was terrified that if she didn't talk fast, Granny might look at her and ask, "Who are you?"

She wanted Granny to remember her home and her family—the good times. Let her forget the terrible journey to the refugee camp and instead remember the farm, the goats, the cow, the chickens, the neat rows of cabbages smiling at the autumn sun. Let her remember her sons, who loved her, and their wives, who took such kind care of her. Let her remember her grandchildren and great-grandchildren playing at her feet and laughing in her lap. But the strangeness of the camp seemed to interfere with those memories. Sometimes Granny thought she was a little girl again. Once she startled Meli by turning to her and saying, her voice pitched high as Vlora's, "Mama, who are all those people?"

❀ ❀ ❀

Meanwhile, NATO bombers were pounding Kosovo. A radio that worked with a crank instead of electricity had been distributed to each tent. Mehmet hardly let anyone else in the family touch the one they had been given. He wound it up and listened to the news every day, so they knew of terrible accidents: NATO bombers striking a column of refugees mistaken for Serbian soldiers, and destroying a train just like the one they'd been herded onto, a train packed with Albanians headed for the border. Many were killed. Mehmet cursed the carelessness of the NATO forces, but Baba just shook his head. "War is madness," he said. "It is the innocent who always suffer most." Once Meli heard him say, half to Mama and half to himself, "Oh, Sevdie, I want to take our children to a place where there is no war." But where on earth was there such a place? Not in Kosovo, not even in Serbia itself. Meli couldn't tell anyone, Baba least of all, the grim satisfaction she took in hearing about the bombs that fell on Serbia. Milosević's people should feel something of the pain they had caused, shouldn't they? They had killed many Kosovar children. Surely it was only right that they should lose children of their own. They should have to pay for the evil they had inflicted.

❄ ❄ ❄

Meli was in the tent when she heard the raucous cheering. She got up quickly and ran outside. It was as though the whole camp had gone crazy. "What is it? What's happening?" she asked, but no one seemed to hear her. She ran to the volleyball area. There was no game going. All the men were half dancing about and shouting. Those who were religious were crying out, *"Alhamdulila!"* Even Baba, who almost never went to a mosque, was joining in the chorus of "God be praised!" with tears running down his cheeks.

She spotted Mehmet and tugged at his sleeve until he turned toward her. "What's happened?" she yelled in his ear.

"You didn't hear? Milosević has surrendered. NATO's won!" Then he dashed off to be in the very middle of the celebration.

Meli walked back to the tent. She sat down in the semi-darkness, hardly listening to the din beyond the tent flap. *Now we can go home.* She said it over and over again in her head and then, to make it real, said it aloud. "Now we can go home at last."

❄ ❄ ❄

There was, of course, no men's chamber available, so later that day Uncle Fadil and Baba and Mehmet met in Baba's tent to hold their discussion. They weren't gone long, but by the time they returned to the rest of the family, who were gathered in the space in front of Uncle Fadil's tent, the little ones were jumping up and down in their excitement, and Meli's heart was fluttering like a caged bird. But when Uncle Fadil spoke, his voice was somber. "We are all eager to go back home, but . . ." He hesitated, and in that space Meli's heart contracted. Uncle Fadil had no home to go back to.

"We don't know what things are like," Baba said. "They say there are land mines and some of the houses left standing may be booby-trapped. Even if it is safe, it will be a hard journey. We'll have to walk, and Granny . . . Well, you can see, it would be too hard for her and the little children . . ."

"Not for me!" Isuf said.

Baba smiled at Isuf, patting his head, as he continued: Considering the hardships and dangers of the trip, only he, Uncle Fadil, and Mehmet would return for now.

Meli saw Mehmet smile. Again he was to be counted among the men.

"We have to see about the store and the apartment. What the situation is, and . . . the farm . . . what we can salvage there. I promise, we will come back as soon as possible. You'll have to wait a little longer, Isuf," Baba said. "It won't be long."

Despite the pleas for patience from the authorities, the Lleshi men were among the thousands who walked out of the camp that June day. The women and children who were left behind stood at the chicken-wire fence and watched them go. After all their determination to stay together, Baba, Mehmet, and Uncle Fadil were leaving them. Meli kept trying to make out the beloved figures, but the three Lleshis were soon lost in the crowd of Albanians flooding out past the gate into the road. They would probably have to walk all the way. Strong as the three of them were, the journey might take several days, and who knew what they would find at the end? It only made sense for the women to stay behind to take care of Granny and the children, and she, Meli, was counted as a woman now. Tomorrow was her thirteenth birthday, not that anyone but she would remember it, and Baba had promised not to be gone long. Then they could all go home.

❉ ❉ ❉

But, oh, it seemed long to those who had been left behind. To Meli it seemed like an eternity. In reality, it was less than two weeks, but when your stomach knots at the thoughts of land mines and booby traps and your whole body is aching with homesickness, a day can feel like years. But Baba, Uncle Fadil, and Mehmet returned to the refugee camp, as Baba had promised.

Before any of the men would speak, the whole family had to be gathered again in the space in front of Uncle Fadil's tent. Meli thought her heart would burst from her chest before Baba finally cleared his throat and began. "We have no idea what has happened to our cousins. They may have fled or . . ." He didn't finish the sentence. "But it's not all bad news. The store and the apartment are still there."

Mehmet glowered. "What the Serbs didn't steal they smashed to pieces."

"At least there are four walls and a roof," Uncle Fadil said, making Mehmet blush. It was clear Uncle Fadil had nothing to go home to.

Baba confirmed this sad truth. "The farmhouse and sheds are destroyed," he said. Then he pulled out something from his pocket and handed it to Mama. "I could only find this little scrap. I think the rest was burned."

Mama rubbed a finger across the piece of what had once been her beloved photo. "My parents," she said. "This was all I had left of them. Why should anyone destroy it?"

"Hate makes no sense," Baba said.

"When are we going home?" Isuf asked the question they were all dying to ask. "I want to go home today. Right now."

"Right now!" echoed Adil.

"Me, too," said Vlora. "Right now."

Baba shook his head sadly. "We have to talk first," he said. Meli sighed, but to her amazement and Mehmet's chagrin Baba told Mehmet to "help watch the little ones" while he and Uncle Fadil asked Mama, Auntie Burbuqe, and Nexima to come with them to Baba's tent.

"What do they have to talk about, Mehmet?" Meli asked. "What is so complicated? If the store and the apartment are there, why can't we just go home?"

"You know Baba. He'll always find something to worry about."

"But the war is over."

Mehmet shrugged. "I think he fears what will happen next."

"What? What can happen now?"

"Don't we need to revenge the evil those pigs have done? Don't we?"

Meli found herself shivering in the summer sun.

❊ ❊ ❊

After what seemed like hours, Uncle Fadil and the women returned. *Where's Baba?* That was the question that no one quite dared ask. Something was up, and from the grim expressions on the faces of the three adults, it was not something they were happy about. Uncle Fadil had somehow gotten some cigarettes, and he sat down and began to smoke. Auntie Burbuqe, Nexima, and Mama pretended there was something inside the tent that needed doing for the twins. Meli looked to Mehmet for some explanation, but he just shrugged. For once he knew as little as she did.

The smaller children had begun a game of tag, racing around several tents. Elez shrieked with pleasure when he was caught, so Isuf made sure that he got caught often, which pleased Vlora and Adil, who never wanted to be "it." It made Meli long to be able to forget everything and play like that. But at thirteen one had to have dignity. *Oh, Baba, where have you gone? What are you doing?*

At last Baba appeared, his face flushed, his eyes bright. He poked his head into the tent. Nexima came out, holding a twin by each hand. They could walk alone now, but it was as though she were escorting them to a solemn meeting. The older women followed her out, and Mama called the children from their play. Baba had everyone sit down in the space in front of Uncle Fadil's tent. The adults sat there, their expressions grim but resolute. Now they were going to hear what had been decided. Meli quickly realized that there would be no arguing, not even from Mehmet, with whatever decision their elders had agreed on. She waited for Baba to speak, never dreaming of the words she would hear.

"As we all know, at present Uncle Fadil and his family have no home to return to. The farm is destroyed, and until things are more settled, it is not wise to try to rebuild. They will go to town, to the apartment, and try to get the store running again. They can take care of Granny and the little children more easily there."

"But what about us?" Isuf asked. "What about our family?"

Baba forced a smile. "Our family? Why, we're headed for a great adventure."

"Adventure?" asked Adil.

"Yes, son, a great adventure. The papers I filled out last month are still in order. We're in line to go to America."

ELEVEN

A Country Far from Home

AMERICA? HOW COULD MELI EVEN IMAGINE IT? OH, SHE HAD seen pictures of Washington and New York on television. But they seemed like cities in science-fiction fantasies to her. She'd never even been to Prishtina, though Nexima and her family had lived there. In her mind America was thin, glamorous women and handsome men, many, many cars, and huge trucks. Maybe there weren't soldiers on the streets or cruel police, but there were lots of criminals, people with guns everywhere, even in the schools. It was a strangely beautiful, dangerous land, and this is where Baba was determined to take them all—to keep them safe! But how could Baba be sure that they would be safe in America? Safer than in Kosovo? She supposed he reckoned that America was far from the threat of those Mehmet had learned so well how to hate. Hatred and the ancient thirst for revenge: that was what Baba feared most. *I'll never tell him how I feel*, she determined. *He mustn't know how much I've come to hate the Serbs.*

To her surprise, Mehmet was not opposed to the idea of America. "I'm going to go to America and get rich. Then I'll come back and fight for independence. Maybe I'll see Bill Clinton. Thank him for the bombs."

They knew that the legendary American president and his wife had come to Macedonia and visited the camp at Stenkovic.

Mehmet felt cheated that he had missed seeing his current hero. "He should have come to our camp to see us," he said.

"But you weren't even here. You were home when he was at Stenkovic," Meli said.

"I'll see him someday."

Someday. All of them, even Meli, frightened as she was by the whole idea of America, were anxious for that "someday" when the word would come and their names would appear on the list of those to leave the camp. The papers had all been filled out. Now they must wait, Baba said, for a sponsor in America: someone who would help them settle into their new country. *But even in a country as rich as America, who would want responsibility for a family with five children,* Meli wondered, *a family in which no one can speak English?*

A few days later Mehmet said that one of the American volunteers had offered to teach English to those who had applied to go to America. Baba was pleased. He insisted that Mehmet and Meli attend. "You should go, too, Baba," Meli said.

Mama agreed. "It is a good example," she said quietly, pointing her chin toward Mehmet. So Baba went with them, but it was a trial for him, Meli saw. Mehmet was so much quicker than their father. *He shouldn't act so smug—just because he's more clever than we are.* She did her best to pretend that she was having just as hard a time as Baba was, though in truth she was catching on much faster than her father.

"Can you tell me the way to the supermarket?" the young volunteer teacher said, and the little class of refugees young and old echoed the alien sounds, all but Baba.

"What does it mean, 'soopera mekit'?" he whispered loudly enough to make several people turn around and stare at him.

"Hush," Mehmet said. "Just repeat."

Baba's sun-browned face couldn't hide the red flush in his cheeks. *When had his mustache turned white? When had so much gray appeared on his head of thick black hair?* Meli bit her lip and fixed her eyes on the instructor.

Meantime, Baba and Uncle Fadil had located a distant relative in Skopje. The Macedonian cousin came to the camp, bringing a gift of money and the loan of an ancient Mercedes. The family that had clung together for so long was about to be torn apart—maybe forever.

"It's time for us to leave," Uncle Fadil said. "Granny is strong enough to travel, and we have the use of this car. I'll stop by and see you when I come back to return it."

Meli held each twin so close they wriggled out of her arms. She hugged Granny and Nexima and dear Auntie Burbuqe, who was sobbing right out loud. They all, except Mehmet—who seemed to think himself too manly to cry—were wiping their eyes when the final good-byes were said. Uncle Fadil shook hands gravely all around. When he got to Mehmet he put his left hand on his nephew's shoulder. "Be a man," he said.

"I'm a man and a half," Mehmet said, and grinned to soften the boast. Uncle Fadil smiled and got in behind the wheel. He looked about, as though he needed to make sure all his passengers were safely in place before starting the engine.

"May your life be lengthened, brother," Baba said, sticking his head in the window of the Mercedes.

Uncle Fadil reached out and touched his older brother's face. "May we see one another well," he replied, his voice cracking before he finished the sentence. Then he revved up the motor of the big car, and they were off. Elez kept his nose to the back window, waving at his cousins, and they all waved back until the car was a dot on the dust of the road. Then, hardly looking at each other, they went back through the camp gate.

"Nobody left but just us chickens," Mehmet said under his breath.

❋ ❋ ❋

Those still in the shrunken camp were all waiting, all wishing to be somewhere else, all checking the list every day to see if their names had magically appeared for transport to a new life. The children had outgrown their clothes, so they went to the designated tent and tried on new ones. Not really new, of course; they were used clothes sent to the camp from people in Western Europe or America. It was silly to hope that the two dresses she chose were stylish, Meli knew. No one would throw away a perfectly good dress if it were up-to-date. Mehmet was thrilled to find a pair of jeans that fit him—well, almost fit. The waist was a little large, but he kept them up with a length of cord. "Jeans," he said proudly. "Just like a Hollywood star."

Fortunately, although July was hot, it was mostly clear. Then, when it did begin to rain, there was no way to keep things dry. The tent smelled of mildew, and the paths were muddy troughs. The family began going barefoot to spare their single pairs of new hand-me-down shoes. They tried to keep clean, but a weekly cold shower did nothing but take off the current layer of mud. As soon as they left the shower tent, they were dirty again. Meli tried not to remember the big enamel tub in the apartment or the luxury of hot water, big bars of soap and bleached white towels, clean underwear, and clothes that fit her body.

By the end of July Baba had stopped going to the classes with them. At first he made excuses about having to check the lists or talk to some camp official about papers, but eventually he didn't bother with excuses. He just didn't go back to class. Meli was secretly relieved. How could she learn anything with Baba at her elbow feeling lost and hopeless and humiliated by his own children? Still, how were they to get along in America if their father couldn't even speak to people? It would be as though Mehmet had become head of the family, and Mehmet wasn't wise and caring like Baba. What would happen to them in that strange new land without him in charge? Why couldn't they just go home? Yes, the apartment would be crowded, though no more crowded than the farmhouse had been last winter. But Baba was adamant: They would wait for the papers and the promise of sponsorship that would let them emigrate to America.

Letters from home, when they came, did not bring good news. Hamza was dead; they were sure of it now. The KLA had confirmed it. Granny stayed in bed all the time. Thank God there was a bed for her to lie in, Uncle Fadil said, for the barbarians had destroyed so much else. Relief teams had brought food, and the NATO troops were trying to keep order, but when the Jokics, their Serb neighbors, fled north, the KLA came and burned their house.

"I asked them," Uncle Fadil wrote, "'Why do you burn a perfectly good house? My cousin and his family could live there when they come back.' But they wouldn't listen to me."

"You see," Baba said when he read them the letter, "hate makes no sense." *Yes, it does, Baba, to everyone but you.* But the thought of the next-door neighbors turning into refugees did not satisfy any need for revenge. The Jokics had done no harm to the Lleshis, or to anyone else that she knew of. And Baba was right: burning a perfectly good house made no sense at all.

Unlike many in the camp, they stayed well. "You see," Mehmet said, "the KLA camp made us strong. If it weren't for them, we'd be sniffling and croaking like these weaklings around here."

"Hush," said Mama. "Thank God for your health, not the KLA."

❋ ❋ ❋

At last came the news they had almost given up hoping for. They were cleared to go to America. They had a sponsor: a church in Vermont.

"Where's Vermont?" Mehmet asked. "Is it near New York?"

Baba wasn't sure, but he didn't think so. America was a very big country.

But a church? "Our sponsors are Christians?" Meli asked.

"Yes," said Baba. "There are many Christians in America."

"Is it safe?" Isuf asked. "All those Christians? Maybe they just want to get us there and kill us."

"And burn down our house!" Adil added.

Meli tried to smile. It was a childish fear, but still . . .

Baba squatted so as to be closer to Isuf's level. "Isuf," he said, "at one time all of us were Christians."

"I was not!"

"Me neither!" said Adil.

"Until the Turks came, we Albanians were all Christians. Skanderbeg was a Christian."

The thought of the great hero whose picture hung in their schoolroom being a Christian was almost too much for the little brothers, who started to protest, but Baba continued. "And there are still Albanian Christians. You remember Mark," he said, mentioning one of their playmates at home. "His mama and baba are Christians."

"They don't go to the Serbian church," Isuf maintained

95

stubbornly. He wasn't about to identify his friend with their enemies.

"No," Baba said, "they go to the Catholic church. There are different kinds of Christians, just as there are different kinds of Muslims. The church that is sponsoring us is still another kind of Christian."

"Not Serbian?"

"No," Baba assured him. "Something else they call Protestant."

"Oh. That's silly," said Isuf.

"Maybe so," said Baba, "but you don't have to be afraid. They want to help us, to be our friends, so you must be very polite to them. All right?"

Isuf nodded. "All right, Baba," he said. "And I'll make Adil and Vlora behave, too."

❀ ❀ ❀

Every day they checked to see if their names were on the list, the list that would tell the time they must be at the gate on the following day for transportation to the airport.

As glad as she would be to leave the discomforts of camp, now that it was almost time to go Meli dreaded the thought of actually leaving. That would mean giving up any hope of going back to her old life. All at once she knew that what she wanted more than anything in the world was the life she had left behind: the homey apartment over Baba's store, her little brothers wrestling in the backyard, Mama making wonderful smells in the kitchen, Mehmet laughing as he teased her. Being best friends with Zana again. And yet, now that permission had actually come for them to emigrate, she found herself growing impatient. If they must go, then they should do so at once.

She was weary of the waiting, tired of being a jailed chicken. If she could not go home, she wanted to be free of her chicken-wire prison.

A few more days of hurrying to get ready, only to be told once again to be patient—there were still details to be worked out—and then one chilly September day, their names appeared on the magic list. The van for the Skopje airport was scheduled for eight a.m. the following morning. They had no watches, so the Lleshis were at the gate at dawn, with the extra clothes they had been given packed into three small plastic suitcases. Baba kept patting his pocket nervously, making sure the precious papers were safe.

"We should have had breakfast," Mama said as they waited. Meli was sure she would have been too nervous to eat, though by the time the van finally appeared, her stomach felt hollow. Baba had been given a little money, and in the airport he bought two sausages and had the woman selling them cut them into pieces so that everyone could have a taste.

"They told me at the camp that there would be food on the airplane," he said. "So just a few bites for now, all right?" The sausage, which was greasy and too highly spiced, lay heavily on Meli's stomach, but she said nothing. Baba was trying so hard to take care of them. If only she had a book, something to read, anything to pass the time. At last the plane was announced. They jumped to their feet and got into the long line of passengers. Another wait, and then they were aboard, three near the window and four in the middle of the huge belly of the plane. The woman in charge showed everyone how to fasten the belts around their waists and what to do if they needed oxygen, and by the time she began to demonstrate how to put on their life preservers if they crashed into the ocean, Meli was in a sweat from anxiety. Finally, though, they were roaring down the field and lifting into the sky, snatched from a world that, however temporary and hard to bear, had felt safe compared to the alien world they were rushing to meet.

"Meli, make Isuf let me sit by the window. It's my turn now." Adil was yanking at the sleeve of her new jacket, which made her realize how hot she felt. She leaned over both boys. There was nothing to see but blue, blue sky and whiteness below. Clouds. Her stomach gave a lurch. They were above the clouds.

"Don't fight, boys," she said, slumping back against the seat.

A uniformed woman—the flight attendant, of course—was leaning over her, saying something in another language. Could it be German? It didn't sound like Macedonian, and it certainly wasn't Albanian or Serbian. Meli shook her head. The attendant tried something else that might have been English. Then why couldn't Meli understand? *Could you tell me the way to the supermarket?* No, of course, that wouldn't do. "Yes," she said. That should be safe.

The woman said something else, maybe in English, indicating the boys. "Yes, yes," Meli said.

The attendant leaned across and put down little shelves from the backs of the seats in front of them. Then on each shelf—or table—she put a napkin and a little package, and she poured each of them a drink. The boys immediately left off fighting and put their noses into the fizz. Yes, it was cola, a rare treat back in the days when they had such a thing as a treat. Meli helped them tear open their strange little packages of mixed salty things and then leaned back once more against the back of the seat.

"Drink it, Meli. It's good," Adil urged.

She obeyed. The boys were loving the airplane. She mustn't spoil it for them. When the real food came, even though her stomach seemed to have been doing flip-flops, she ate everything. Who knew when the next meal might be? And, although she couldn't have believed she'd be able to sleep, once the attendant showed her how to lower the back of her seat, she dropped off.

Baba was shaking her. "We have to get off," he said.

"Is it New York?"

"No, Vienna. We change to another plane here. Wake up the boys."

They clung to Baba like baby monkeys. They weren't going to lose each other in Vienna. They'd never find each other again in that huge, crowded airport where no one spoke any language that any of them knew. Mehmet showed off his English, and he proudly herded them to the transfer gate that said NEW YORK JFK. Again the wait, the line, the moving down the narrow aisle into the broad belly of the plane to find their seats. Like a veteran of air travel, Meli helped her little brothers fasten their seat belts and then fastened her own and sat back. *This is it. In a few more hours, we will be in New York, USA.*

TWELVE

America

NEW YORK. WELL, SHE THOUGHT, AS SHE STAGGERED SLEEP-ily off the plane, they had nothing anyone would want to steal—that was a plus of sorts. Baba and Mehmet carried the plastic suitcases of hand-me-down clothes they had been given at the camp. They were so small that there had been no need to check them as luggage.

"Meli, watch out for your brothers," Baba said.

Mama had Vlora by the hand, and Meli reached out for Isuf and Adil. Isuf started to resist, but one look from Baba and he took Meli's hand. She held on to both boys as the whole family went down the endless corridor to the huge hall, where it looked as though hundreds of people were lined up, all waiting to be let into America. Vlora was so sleepy that she was falling down, so Baba gave the suitcase he was carrying to Mama and picked her up. She nestled against his neck, dead to the world.

More waiting, until at last they reached the white line painted on the floor and were waved over to a tall booth, behind which sat a grim, uniformed guard. They crowded around Baba as he handed over the papers he had been given at the camp. It took time, because the officer had to send for someone who could talk to Baba in Albanian. It seemed to Meli that it was taking far too much time. Maybe the papers were counterfeit and Baba would be thrown in jail and . . .

"Is something wrong, Meli?"

"No, Isuf," she said, breathing deeply to make herself calm. "These things always take time." Though how did she know? She hoped her brother wouldn't ask.

It seemed forever, but eventually they were all pointed toward the gigantic customs hall, where they didn't have to wait for luggage, as they had only their three tiny suitcases. They had nothing of worth to declare—Mehmet said that someone at the camp had told him to look for the Nothing to Declare sign. The two guards there were busy talking to each other, but one of them stopped long enough to glance at the family and nod toward the doorway. They were blinking like little moles in sunlight when they exited the hall and found themselves in the reception area, where hundreds of people were pressing against the ropes, all waiting for their family or friends to emerge.

"They told me at the camp that someone would meet us here," Baba said, worriedly scanning the people at the barrier who were waving and calling to other arrivals.

"Look!" said Isuf. They all turned and saw a woman standing near the rope with a piece of cardboard that said LLESHI. Still tightly bunched together, they moved down the ramp, around the barrier, and toward the sign. Baba bowed. "We are the Lleshi family," he said, and, miraculously, he was answered in Albanian by the woman holding the sign.

"I'm glad to see you," she said. "Did you have a good trip?"

"We had cola!" Adil said.

"Thank you," said Baba. "A very smooth trip."

"I'm sure you're tired," the woman said, "but we have to go to another terminal. Your plane for Vermont leaves in just over an hour, and if you miss it, it will be a very long wait for the next flight." She smiled at them. "So, are we ready to go?"

They were getting on a third plane? This was another endless journey—like fleeing the Serbs—only this time they could do it sitting down with food served on little trays. *What is it like in Vermont, Baba?* Meli wanted to ask, but she couldn't. They were walking too fast, and she had to be sure she stayed close and held on to Adil and Isuf. And then, of course, how could Baba know what Vermont was like?

They rode a moving staircase—the little boys loved that!—and took a bus to another building, where they came to a barrier. Their escort said something about Baba's papers to the woman in uniform who was checking tickets and identity cards. "I can't go past security with you," she said, "but wait here a minute. I'll get an airline representative to take you to the right gate."

"Hmmph," grunted Mehmet. "We can count, can't we? Surely we can find the gate."

"Hush," said Mama. "She only means to be kind."

But the airline person did treat them like children, Meli thought, herding them through the metal detector and to their new gate, finding them seats in the waiting area, motioning for them not to move until—she pointed at a person standing behind a high desk and mimed someone talking into a microphone. She raised her eyebrows in a question.

"Yes," said Mehmet in exaggerated English. "We un-der-stand. We will wait."

Her eyes widened a bit, but she didn't say anything, just gave a little wave and disappeared.

"They all think we're idiots," said Mehmet.

"We should have said 'Sank you,'" Meli said.

"It's 'Thhhh-anku you,'" Mehmet corrected.

"Come, come," said Baba. "Time to get on." Meli could see him counting heads, though they were all within inches of each other.

This was a much smaller plane, and they weren't all sitting in a row together. Meli was with Adil, Mehmet with Isuf, Mama with Vlora, and Baba was all alone way at the back. Meli found herself turning and looking down the aisle to make sure he was still there.

There was no real food on the trip from New York to Vermont. Adil was delighted to get cola and a little packet of salty bits. He finished his drink in a few gulps. Meli took sips of her cola, feeling both exhausted and jumpy. She was so tired of traveling, every minute taking her farther and farther from home.

"Can I have the rest?" Adil asked.

"What?"

"Your cola. If you don't want it, I do."

She pushed it over toward him. Her legs were longing for a bed—somewhere she could stretch out fully. Somewhere she could sleep for days.

Finally, they stumbled off the small plane and followed the crowd down the hall to the security barrier—no passports needed here, it seemed.

"Will there be welcomers?" Adil asked, gripping her hand so tightly that it hurt.

"I don't know," she said. "I hope so."

Outside the barrier there were four people waiting together in a little bunch, one of them holding a sign that read in Albanian WELCOME TO THE LLESHI FAMILY. She thought for one happy moment that the sign meant that Adil's "welcomers" could speak Albanian. Baba did, too, evidently, because he greeted them formally in Albanian and began to introduce the family.

"No! No!" they said, waving their hands in protest. And that was all the English Meli could understand, even though the welcomer holding the sign went on to say something very slowly and loudly, his mouth painfully cramped around every syllable.

Before Mehmet could mutter something sarcastic, Meli stepped forward. "Hello," she said in her best English. "I come from Kosovo. My name is Meli Lleshi. What, please, is your name?"

To her dismay, no one answered. They just kept shaking their heads and smiling. The man holding the sign kept looking toward the doors of the small airport.

"Ask them about the toilets," Mama whispered.

Mehmet tried, but the people just kept smiling and nodding.

"Idiots," said Mehmet. "Don't they understand their own language?"

Finally, the outside glass doors slid open, and a woman came running up to the group. She seemed to be apologizing to them. Then she turned to the family. "I'm sorry I'm late," she said in perfect Albanian. "I will translate for you."

"Where are the toilets?" Mama asked.

The translator guided Mama, Meli, and Vlora to the women's toilet. The man with the sign took Baba and the boys to the men's.

"No wonder I couldn't see them," Mehmet muttered to Meli when she rejoined the men. "They call them 'rest rooms,' as if you took a nap in there."

Two of the welcomers had disappeared. "They've gone to get the cars," said the translator, whose name was Adona. "I guess you have no other luggage."

Mehmet opened his mouth, but Baba grabbed his arm, so he shut it again. "We have a new life now," Baba said. "Everything will be new."

"Yes," said Adona. She may have sighed. Meli couldn't be sure.

The smiling, nodding Americans put Mama, Vlora, and Meli into the backseat of one large, silver car, and Baba, Mehmet, and the little boys into a green van. Adona climbed into the van as well. The welcomers split up, a man and a woman in each vehicle, and then they took off, pausing only to pay someone at the exit of the airport. There didn't seem to be any police on guard. There wasn't a soldier or a gun in sight.

Meli tried not to panic. She told herself it wasn't Kosovo—people didn't just disappear in America—but she kept turning to look out the back window to keep the van in sight, just in case.

Thankfully, the man and woman in the front seat didn't try to talk to them. Occasionally, they would say something quietly to each other. Once in a while the woman in the passenger seat would turn and smile at them. Mama and Meli would try to smile back.

Vlora, now wide awake, was staring out the window. "Look!" she cried. Meli looked and saw, to her astonishment, mountains. She felt a great wave of homesickness for her own Cursed Mountains and the Sharr range with its high pastures where horses ran free. Was the family free now? She looked at the backs of the welcomers' heads and wondered.

The car ride was nearly as long as the last plane ride had been. They left the broad highway and took a more winding road down a hill into a town. They turned off the street lined with shops onto another lined with large trees. The leaves were beginning to change color like the—no, not like the chestnuts in the hills.

At last the car—and then, thankfully, the van—pulled up in front of a huge house. As they got out of the car, Adona came over to explain that they would have an apartment in the house, not the whole house. Mama smiled and nodded. They walked up one flight of stairs behind the welcomers. Someone produced a key, opened the door, and then handed the key to Baba.

"Welcome home," he said, or at least that's what Meli thought he said. Adona didn't bother to translate it. The Lleshis took off their shoes and walked across the threshold. Adona said something to the welcomers, so they took off their shoes as well, looking a bit embarrassed as they stood there in their stocking feet.

For Meli the apartment lacked the welcoming feel of home, but it was far better than a tent. She meant to thank the big, smiling Americans, but she was too tired to make the effort of putting her tongue between her teeth to make the right sounds, and when Adona showed her the little room where she and Vlora were meant to sleep, she fell like a rock on the nearest bed and was asleep before the welcoming party left the apartment.

THIRTEEN

Strangers in a Strange Land

BABA COULDN'T HAVE REALIZED HOW TIRED THEY WERE, OR he would never have made the children start school at once. Meli's head was still spinning from lack of sleep and the change in time, but even if she'd been rested and acclimated, the first days at the new school still would have been totally confusing.

One of the welcomers, as Adil had named the church people, drove Meli and Mehmet to the high school the second morning after they arrived. It helped that Adona went with them to fill out papers and answer questions and take home the things that their father was supposed to sign.

"It will be fine," she said as she started to leave. "You'll adjust in no time."

Meli watched her go. Now what was she supposed to do? The woman in the office motioned them to chairs and then went back to her desk, which was behind a high counter. Mehmet and Meli sat down and watched the big clock on the wall. It was about an hour before someone came into the office, spoke briefly to the woman behind the counter, and then turned to them.

Very slowly, in English they could almost understand, she said, "I am the English teacher for international students."

"Hello," said Mehmet, jumping to his feet and pumping her

outstretched hand up and down. "I am Mehmet Lleshi. I come from Kosovo. I am Albanian."

"I am glad to meet you, Mehmet," the teacher said. "I am Missus ——" But Meli couldn't understand the name.

"This girl is my sister. Her name is Meli. Also name is Lleshi," said Mehmet in English, and then under his breath in Albanian, "Stand up and shake hands."

Meli stood up.

"I am happy to meet you, Meli." The teacher held out her hand.

Meli shook it, her eyes on the new sneakers one of the welcomers had given her.

"Come with me."

At least that is what she seemed to be saying. They followed her down the hall and up two flights of stairs, then down another hall to a small room off what seemed to be a library. There was a cardboard sign on the door: ESL. The teacher pointed to the letters one by one. "E-S-L. English as a Second Language," she explained.

"Or third," muttered Mehmet. But since Meli hadn't understood the teacher, she didn't know what Mehmet meant, either.

The teacher pointed to the chairs around a table in the middle of the room and seemed to be inviting them to sit down. Mehmet did at once, so Meli sat as well, hoping she could stay awake. It would be terribly rude to fall asleep in front of a teacher on her first day.

They spent most of that day in the room with the ESL teacher. She gave them each a map of the enormous school— three floors of it, mostly classrooms, but also an auditorium, cafeteria, library, and two gymnasiums. Meli looked at the map. Who ever heard of a school so large that you needed a map to find your way around it? She thought longingly of the one room in the old house that had been school before, and of Zana sitting close beside her at their double desk.

"Pay attention," Mehmet said in her ear.

She shook off her thoughts and tried to listen to the teacher. The woman was taking their class schedules and writing down what time they were to go to each class and marking in red on the map the time they were to be in that particular place. Meli couldn't really follow what the teacher was saying, although the woman seemed to be trying hard to speak slowly and point out or act out—as in the case of the cafeteria and library and gymnasium—what they were to be doing in the various locations. All Meli wanted to do was take a nap, but Mehmet seemed to be following everything she said quite closely, nodding as though he understood every word.

At some point a bell rang, and soon the door opened and five students, all of whom appeared to be Asian, came laughing and talking into the room. They all looked very American in their blue jeans and sweatshirts with big letters on the front. Meli pulled her dress over her knees and buttoned the front of her wool cardigan. She must look very peculiar to these students, who seemed so happy and at home in this new country.

The teacher was talking. Meli must pay attention. "These are our new friends." *Did she say "friends"?*

"Hello," said Mehmet formally. "I am Mehmet Lleshi. I come from Kosovo. I am Albanian. This is my sister. Her name is Meli Lleshi." He glared at Meli. So Meli tried to smile.

The others grinned and nodded. "Meli, Mehmet. I want you to meet . . ." And then Missus whatever-her-name-was said everyone else's name. It was all a jumble to Meli. She was relieved when the teacher started the lesson for the class.

Mehmet was listening carefully. He didn't try to participate, but Meli was sure her brother knew exactly what was going on—unlike Meli herself, whose head was pounding with exhaustion and confusion.

※ ※ ※

The first weeks were pure torture for Meli. Even when a teacher was kind enough to ask another student to make sure Meli got to her next class, she felt lost and alone in that gigantic place. *Oh, Zana, I wish you were here.*

The only time she saw Mehmet at school was in the ESL class, and he was so intent on learning English as quickly as possible that he had no time for her. If she dared complain about anything, he would pretend not to understand her. "Speak English, Meli. It's the only way to learn."

She tried to speak, but the effort was too great. She gave up and simply listened. She envied the little ones. They not only chattered away at school, but they played with neighborhood children after school and on the weekends. They could translate for Mama and Baba before Mehmet could. It made him so angry that he studied ten times harder. He listened to the radio or watched TV when he wasn't actually studying. "To get the pronunciation right. You have to get the pronunciation or they laugh." Mehmet couldn't stand to be laughed at. His younger brothers and Vlora just laughed right back when the neighborhood children laughed at them. Besides, the pronunciation seemed easy for them.

Mama shook her head. "They're forgetting Albanian," she said.

But if English was hard for Meli, it seemed almost impossible for Mama and Baba. They went to a course at the library three mornings a week, but they refused to speak in public. If they needed to go to the grocery store or post office, they always took one of the children to translate for them.

The biggest problem for them all was Baba. He needed to get a job, but what job could a middle-aged man do? One who was hopeless in English?

"What kind of work did you do in Kosovo?" Mr. Craven, one of the welcomers, asked.

"He owned a food market," Mehmet answered.

"Oh," said Mr. Craven, and the tone of the "oh" meant that Baba's previous occupation was of no help in his new situation. With no English, he could not even clerk in someone else's grocery store. Finally, after weeks of trudging the streets and standing in line at the employment office, Mr. Craven found a little downtown restaurant that needed a dishwasher. The owner agreed to give Baba a try. Adona went with him the first day so that she could help the owner explain everything to Baba. From then on, he was on his own. A little of the old Baba shone through when he told the children about his new job. "The church people agreed to sponsor us only until we could get settled," he said. "We have to begin taking responsibility for ourselves." Still, even working long hours every day, his pay was poor—not nearly enough after taxes to pay the family bills—so they remained dependent on the welcomers. Meli liked "welcomers" better than "church people." That reminded her too much of the Serbs.

It was hard to explain American things to Baba. Although Adona had told the welcomers about taking off shoes when they came into Leshis' apartment, sometimes they forgot. It was very hard for Baba not to look shocked when some big American tromped around with the same shoes on that he had worn in the street.

"It's the American way, Baba," Mehmet said. "They don't mean to be rude."

Baba would shake his head. "It's a very strange way," he said.

Even stranger was trying to tell Baba about Hell-o-ween. The younger children had come home from school all excited about dressing up and putting on masks and touring the neighborhood for gifts of candy—especially the candy part.

"No," said Baba. "Absolutely not. Even if we are poor, we do not beg."

"Everybody does it," Isuf said. "Not just poor children. Everyone."

"Baba," Mehmet said, "it's like in Kosovo when the children ask for candy on the holidays. No different."

"What kind of people hide their faces? Only people who plan bad things—people who are ashamed of what they are doing. Not my family. Not my children. No."

The men who burned the farm hid their faces, thought Meli, but she hoped by now Isuf had forgotten that day.

"And," Isuf went on stubbornly, "we have to buy candy to give to the children who come here."

"We have no money for candy," Baba said. "Not even for our own children."

Isuf was beside himself. "If we don't go out and we don't give candy, what will I say at school? People will think we don't know about Hell-o-ween."

"People will be right. We don't know," said Baba.

"Maybe," Mama said quietly, "we should find out about this strange holiday."

Mehmet did and learned that on Main Street all the stores gave out candy to children on Hell-o-ween afternoon. "But it's called 'Halloween,' not 'Hell-o-ween.' And no one thinks it's

112

begging. I'll take the boys and Vlora downtown while you're at work."

"No masks!" Baba said.

The children didn't care about the masks. They were so thrilled to be allowed to take part in the candy collecting. Mehmet gave each of them a little bag that was filled to the brim in less than half an hour. Then he marched them home.

"Now," he said, "each of you must give me your candy."

Adil groaned.

"Why?" asked Vlora.

"You always want to tell everyone what to do," complained Isuf.

"If it weren't for me, you wouldn't have any candy. Now hand it over. We have to save some to give away tonight, and the rest we'll put in a jar and it will last a long time."

❅ ❅ ❅

The next holiday was something called Thanksgiving, but they were allowed to take part without argument, as Baba approved of thanking God for their safety and health and shelter and food. They were invited to a huge dinner at one of the local churches—not the one that their welcomers had come from, but some of them were there anyway, dishing out plates of turkey and potatoes and green beans and something they called "stuffing" and a bright red sweet gelatin that went with the meat. Then afterward they had pie and coffee.

"When do they thank God?" Baba asked Mehmet.

"At the beginning, when people shut their eyes, that was it."

"They don't kneel to pray here?"

Mehmet shrugged. "They don't make so much of prayers here," he said.

❄ ❄ ❄

Christmas, Baba had heard of. How could you live among Christians and not hear of it? Again, though, there didn't seem to be much religion in it.

"What is Santa Claus going to bring me, Baba?" Vlora asked.

"I don't know this Santa Claus person."

Once more, Mehmet took charge. He wheedled a little money from Mama and got the younger children presents "from Santa Claus": a tiny doll for Vlora and a soccer ball for Isuf and Adil to share. It was hardly enough to brag about to their friends, but it was something, and Meli was grateful that Mehmet cared enough to make them feel included in the American celebrations. The welcomers came with gifts: warm socks, gloves for the older members of the family and mittens for the younger, winter caps, and a ham for their Christmas dinner so big that it lasted a month. They hadn't eaten pork in Kosovo—it was against Muslim customs—but somehow in this land of strangeness it felt fitting.

Then it was 2000, a new year, a new century, a new millennium. All the terror and loss the family had endured since the day of the pelican were in the past. All the wars and oppression that their nation had suffered were of another age. "Everything is new!" Baba declared. "*Alhamdulila!* God be praised!"

❄ ❄ ❄

Meli found she was actually getting used to school. She didn't know for sure when the torrents of noise broke into sentences that actually made sense to her, but by her fourteenth birthday in June, English was no longer the headache-making racket it had been in September. Her ears had become accustomed to its

114

strange sounds, and the new words began to feel far less clumsy in her mouth. There was a special school term in the summer for people who needed to catch up. The days were hot and the building was not air-conditioned, but her old school had been even hotter. The classes were small, and she could understand almost everything that went on. It was only when the other students talked and joked among themselves that she had trouble following.

As for Mehmet, he had discovered that there was a group of boys who gathered every afternoon on the school soccer field to play. At first he just stood and watched, but soon he joined in, so Meli would go on home without him. He would return later, his face flushed, his eyes wide with excitement. It was a real regulation field with good, almost new balls, and the other boys were skilled enough to provide a challenge. "Of course, I am the best," he declared.

Mr. Marcello, the high school boys' soccer coach, stopped by one afternoon to watch the boys play. When the game was breaking up, he called Mehmet over and asked him to try out for the regular team.

❀ ❀ ❀

One afternoon in August, when the boys' team had begun its fall practice, Meli took Isuf and Adil over to the school to watch Mehmet and his teammates. She tried not to gaze across the school grounds to the distant field where the girls' team was practicing. If only she had been allowed to play at home. It looked like so much fun, and here girls could play, too. But she'd never learned; she'd only watched.

"Look, Meli, over there. Those are girls."

"I know, Isuf. They have a girls' team, too."

"Really? Then why don't you play?"

"I don't know how."

"Yes, you do. You've watched millions of times. You could do it." Then, without another word, Isuf took off running toward the far field.

She shaded her eyes, trying to see where he had gone.

"He's talking to somebody," Adil said. "Is he supposed to talk to strangers?"

"I think it's a teacher, Adil. It's okay."

"I think we'd better check on him."

She took his hand and walked over to the other field. Isuf was talking animatedly to a woman.

"She's the coach, Adil. It's okay. She's a teacher."

Adil let go of Meli's hand and ran over to his brother. Both the coach and Isuf turned to see where Adil was pointing, and then they followed him to where Meli stood.

"Your brother tells me you might be a soccer player," she said.

Meli shook her head. "No, it's my older brother who is the soccer player. Not me."

"But if your brother is such a fine player, I suspect you might have some talent as well. How about coming tomorrow and trying out for us?"

Meli's heart began to pound. *What if . . . ?* "I don't think my father would . . . I mean, in our family, girls don't . . ."

"Would you like for me to call him?"

Meli shook her head. "He doesn't speak English . . . well, not yet. He's studying."

"I'll ask him!" Isuf said.

"No," said the coach, giving Isuf a pat on the head, "I think we'd better leave it up to Meli to ask."

Isuf, however, couldn't contain his excitement. As soon as

116

they got in the door, he went running to Mama. "Guess what!" he cried. "Guess what!"

"I'm not so good at guessing." Mama was cooking supper. She stuck the tip of her finger in the dish, licked it, and sighed. "Never the right ingredients here. It doesn't taste right, whatever I do."

"Your food is always good, Mama," Meli said. "What do you want me to do to help?"

"Tell her, Meli. Tell her what the teacher said."

Now Mama was paying attention. "What did the teacher say? Is something wrong?"

"No. It's fine."

"Go on, Meli. Tell her!"

"Tell me what?" Mama asked.

"The teacher, the coach—her name is Mrs. Rogers—well . . ."

Now Mama had both hands on her hips. "Yes?"

"She wants me to ask Baba if I can join the soccer team."

Mama shook her head. "He won't have you playing a boys' game."

"They have two teams, Mama. One is all boys—that's Mehmet's team—and the other is only for girls."

"They don't play together?"

"No, Mama, it's entirely separate."

"Oh. I never heard of this. Just in America, huh?"

"No. I've seen it on television. Girls play in a lot of countries."

"Is that so?"

"But if you think it is better not to ask Baba . . ."

Mama went back to her cooking. "He has so many worries right now. He works so hard and has so little money. Granny is so frail. We don't know if she lives or dies."

"I won't ask, Mama. It's all right."

"But Mama, the teacher told her to ask Baba. She *has* to ask Baba," Isuf said.

"Did the teacher tell you to ask?"

"It's all right, Mama. I don't even know how to play. I've only just watched the boys."

Mama left the stove and came to Meli. She took Meli's face in both her hands. They were rough and warm. "Is this something you would like to do, my dear one?"

"Yes, Mama."

"Then we will ask your baba."

At first Baba said no, sports were for boys. Girls should help their mothers, not run around panting and yelling and kicking balls at each other.

"You said yourself, Hashim, that this is America. It is a place of new beginnings. Things are different here. Why don't we let our Meli try . . . see if she likes soccer . . . see if she is good enough to play on a team just for girls."

"Would it make you happy, Meli?" he asked.

"Yes, Baba. I'd like to try."

"Your mama says you should try." He shrugged his shoulders. "So I will agree."

She went to the practice the very next day. Mrs. Rogers gave her a practice uniform. "I can't pay," Meli said.

"It's an old one. Don't worry."

Her legs were strong, and she could run as fast as any of the others. Mrs. Rogers kept her afterward every day to help her with dribbling and passing, and to make sure she had all the rules clear in her head. Soon she was playing forward. She had never felt quite so free as she did racing down the field, her hair flying behind her. *This is how the wild horses feel*, she thought.

118

FOURTEEN

A New Year

MELI WAS EAGER FOR SCHOOL TO BEGIN. MRS. ROGERS HAD assured her that she would be on the junior varsity soccer team and most likely make it to the varsity by the following year. She didn't mind being on the junior squad. It meant she got to play every day in practice, and she was making friends—well, maybe just a friend. Rachel, who played sweeper, was shy, but she always smiled at Meli, and once she even congratulated her when Meli put a goal past Brittany, the varsity goalkeeper.

When classes began, none were easy, but they were much easier than they had been in the spring and summer. Meli nearly always understood the assignments, and she worked hard on them. The ESL teacher was quite willing to go over her papers and point out grammatical errors, and even though English was a crazy language, refusing to obey its own rules and often making no sense at all, Meli just gritted her teeth and made the corrections.

Mehmet had little difficulty with his schoolwork. He was whizzing through advanced algebra, and he seemed to glide through even the courses that demanded lots of English knowledge. He was already on the boys' varsity soccer squad. But Meli couldn't help noticing, on the days when the junior varsity girls went over to watch the boys' games, that he still walked alone, like a cat in the night. There was something bristly about her brother that the other boys sensed. They played soccer with him. They won games because of him, but they never carried Mehmet from the field on their shoulders. She didn't dare say anything about it to him, but surely he was aware of it. Couldn't he relax, just a little? Couldn't he try to smile when someone else on the team made a goal?

As much as she worried about Mehmet, she worried more about their father. Yes, he'd been given a tiny raise at his dish-washing job, but the welcomers were still helping with the rent. The family had a government card for food, and when Vlora got an ear infection that winter, Mrs. Craven from the church went with Mama and Adona to the doctor's, and the welcomer made sure Mama didn't have to pay anything over and above the government help.

Mama had been humiliated. The card for food was bad enough, but not being able to go alone to the doctor with her child? Not being able to pay? She talked to Adona, and by January Mama was working during the day at a motel, cleaning rooms and making up beds for travelers. You didn't have to know English to clean rooms. Baba hated it, but what could he say? They needed more money.

Meli came home from school every afternoon to take care of the younger ones and cook dinner. Mehmet was playing basketball. He hadn't made varsity, which was his dream, but he got a place on the junior squad by sheer determination. Next year he would be varsity, he vowed, and in the spring he would go out for the track team so he would be in good shape for soccer. *Why doesn't Baba ask him to get a job after school and help with all the expenses? He is old enough.* But no, Baba didn't suggest it, and Meli didn't dare.

❊ ❊ ❊

The Vermont winter was cold, but all Meli had to do was remember how cold they had been at the camp in the hills, where there had been no place to come into to get warm. And then, finally, after the snows and the mud, it was spring again—the Vermont hillsides so green they dazzled her eyes. It was just two years ago that they had left the farm and fled across the hills of eastern Kosovo to the refugee camp in Macedonia. She was suddenly aware of a homesickness that in the excitement and craziness of the time in Vermont she had been able to push deep below the surface. She looked at the mountains and thought of the mountains of home. All of a sudden, English sounded harsh and discordant compared to the melody of her native tongue. She missed Auntie Burbuqe's bread and soup and the giggles of the twins. And, oh, how she missed Zana. She had written a letter to Zana, but there had been no reply. Meli and Rachel often ate lunch together and sometimes helped each other with homework, but she couldn't tell Rachel about the things that mattered most to her—the things she loved or feared, the things she hated.

She didn't even tell Rachel when it was her birthday. She turned fifteen two days before the end of the semester. Back home Mehmet had thought that when he turned fifteen he would truly be a man, and she did feel more adult somehow, though Mehmet himself still treated her like a child. Mama made a cake and Vlora taught them all to sing an American birthday song. The younger Leshis could hardly keep from giggling when Mama and Baba kept singing "Happy burrs-day" to dear Meli.

There was no need to go to summer school this year. She and Mehmet were performing as well as most of their classmates—

121

often, in Mehmet's case, surpassing them. *Now, maybe, Mehmet will get a job—at least until soccer practice begins.* But no, there were always pickup games of basketball or soccer. He left the house right after breakfast. Some days he didn't bother to come home for lunch.

Meli was fully in charge of the apartment. Mama cooked breakfast, but both she and Baba left for work as soon as they had eaten. Meli coaxed the boys and Vlora to help her clean up, and then they all went outdoors. If it wasn't too hot, they went to the playground near the elementary school. It was a long walk, and often Meli packed sandwiches and a big bottle of water so they could picnic in the shade of a tree. She took a book for herself. There were no books in Albanian, of course, but now she could read English well enough to enjoy almost any book she chose from the free library.

It was wonderful to be able to borrow books. She always got some for the young ones, too. The boys were good readers now and Vlora, at seven, was quickly improving, but Meli loved picking out books to read aloud to her sister. Vlora drank in every word and often stroked the beautiful pictures as though they were living things. On very hot days they would spend whole hours in the cool stone library building, reading. No one ever asked them to leave.

In August, when soccer practice began, Meli took the children with her and made them sit on the sidelines and watch. Sometimes the boys would wander over to the other field, where Mehmet's team was practicing. They were very proud of their big brother. He was so obviously the star. Meli wasn't a star, but Mrs. Rogers told her that she had improved enough to make varsity. Despite everything, this was going to be the best year of her life.

If only the news from Kosovo were better. Uncle Fadil had written that Granny was too weak now to sit up in bed. She was refusing to eat even the healing broths that Auntie Burbuqe made just for her. The last week of August, the dreaded letter arrived. Granny had simply turned her face to the wall and died. Uncle Fadil had borrowed a truck so that they could take her home and bury her in a field near the ruins of the farmhouse.

Baba dropped the letter to the floor and began to sob. The family stood watching helplessly. They had never seen their father shed more than a few tears. He was the strong one. But there he sat, bent over, his face in his hands, his whole body shaking. "I should have been there," he said. "A son should be with his mother when she dies." Yes, they all should have been there. *Damn those Serbs.*

The next day Baba and Mama went to work as usual, Mehmet and Meli went to soccer practice, and the children played with the neighbors. *How can life just go on as though nothing has happened?* But it did—at least the motions of life went on, even when the heart felt hollow.

FIFTEEN

9/11

A T FIRST IT WAS ONLY A RUMOR. THEN THE MATH TEACHER announced it in class. Airplanes full of passengers had crashed into the two tallest buildings in New York City, and another had smashed the huge military headquarters in Washington, DC. America was under attack.

"But who did it?" a boy blurted out.

"We don't know yet," the teacher said. Her voice was quiet, but Meli could hear the quaver in it. "The radio said 'terrorists.'"

"What terrorists?"

"We don't know any details. But we mustn't panic. If we are at war, we will all have to be brave and clear-headed. I've been asked to announce that we will complete the school day but that there will be no after-school activities. No sports practices or clubs. Everyone is to go straight home after the last bell."

Meli could hardly breathe. She could see in the eyes of her classmates a mixture of excitement and fear. She felt only dread. She knew what war was like. Had they fled Kosovo only to be plunged into the midst of its horrors in America?

❀ ❀ ❀

At home they watched on television as the plane hit the second tower, over and over again, and as both towers crumbled to giant piles of debris, over and over again. Their throats were dry. They could not speak or look at each other. "Turn it off," Baba commanded. He had been sent home from work early. No one had come to the restaurant. Everyone in America was at home watching the planes crash and the towers fall. Did they eat that night? They must have, but afterward Meli couldn't remember eating, just the replay of the planes crashing and the towers falling. Even with the screen black, the image of the disaster played on in her mind.

After Vlora and the younger boys were put to bed, Mehmet turned the TV on again. That was when they heard the news that the whole world now knew: The terrorists who had crashed the planes into the Twin Towers and blown open the Pentagon were all Muslims. Baba shook his head in disbelief. "This is not the way of the Prophet," he said. "This is sickness, madness."

The next day, going to her locker, Meli realized that people were staring at her, and that after she passed knots of students in the halls there was silence and then a whispered exchange. She was used to people not speaking to her, but this was different. *Everyone is upset. We're all afraid.* A number of people had stayed home, fearing somehow that the terrorists would find their way to Vermont and bomb the largest building in their town, which was the high school.

The principal announced over the PA system that classes and activities would go on as usual. But nothing felt usual. During soccer practice no one passed her the ball. She tried to pretend that she didn't notice the strange looks sent her way. Once, she found herself sprawling on the field. No one had meant to trip her, had they? But later, as she showered, she could hear one of the seniors talking. It was Brittany, the varsity goalkeeper. She seemed to be talking loudly on purpose, so that Meli couldn't help but hear her over the noise of the water.

"That's what her family is," Brittany was saying. "She's one of *them*. Her and that weird brother of hers."

"No," someone protested. "She's okay."

"Just ask her," Brittany said. "You'll see."

Should she just stay in the shower, pretend she'd heard nothing? But that seemed cowardly. Meli turned off the water, wrapped her towel around herself, and stepped out into the locker room. It was as if someone had pushed the mute button. No noise. Just stares.

Brittany, the only fully dressed girl in the room, gave Rachel a shove. "Go ahead, ask her." Rachel, who had been trying to pull on her jeans, nearly fell on her face. She caught her balance and then glanced back at Brittany before turning, red-faced, toward Meli. "Someone said you were one of them, Meli," she said, her voice hardly more than a whisper. "That's not true, is it?"

"What do you mean, 'them'?" Meli asked. "I don't understand." She looked from one team member to another. "If you mean what nationality, I am Kosovar."

"But what's that?" Brittany asked. "It's not *Christian*, is it?"

"No." Her throat was so tight that she could hardly speak. "No. Serbs are Christian. I am not a Serb. I—my family—is Albanian."

"I thought you just said 'Kosovar.'" Brittany's eyes narrowed to a slit.

"Yeah, Meli." It was Chrystal, the junior whose place Meli had taken on the varsity squad. "What are you *really*?"

"I told you. I am Albanian Kosovar."

"Come on, Meli." Brittany stepped around Rachel and glared at Meli. "You *are* one of them. You know you are."

"Explain what you mean, 'them.'" Of course, by now Meli knew full well what Brittany and the others meant by "them," but she wanted to make Brittany say it out loud, to her face. "How am I one of *them?*" She leaned so close to Brittany that she could see the pimples on the girl's cheeks set to explode.

Brittany straightened. "Like the terrorists." She stepped back slightly. "You know, like their religion."

"I'm not a religious person." Meli walked over toward her locker and opened it.

"I told you she wasn't a Christian."

"I am not a religious person," Meli continued, keeping her eyes on her locker and her voice as steady as she could. "But if I have to choose Christian or Muslim, then, okay, I am Muslim." She turned around. "But that doesn't make me one of *them.* I am not a terrorist."

Brittany shoved Rachel forward once more. Meli wrapped her towel more tightly around herself and looked into the face of the girl she had thought of as a friend. Rachel looked everywhere except at Meli.

"Ask her about her brother, Rachel," Brittany demanded. "Ask if he's a terrorist."

"It is not terrorist to want to fight for your homeland!" As soon as the words were out of her mouth, Meli knew she should never have said them. Rachel backed away, her eyes wide.

"See?" Brittany yelled so loud her voice reverberated around the tiles. "See? I told you!" She whirled around toward her locker. Opening the door, she grabbed her book bag and threw it over her shoulder before she turned again toward Meli. "Why don't you and your brother just go back to where you came

127

from? We don't want any Muslim terrorists around here." With that she slammed her locker shut and marched out of the locker room.

For a few moments they all stared at the door as it swung behind Brittany, and then, careful not to look Meli's way, everyone finished dressing quickly and left, leaving Meli standing there alone, shivering in her towel.

Pull yourself together. Get dressed. Go home. She was thinking in Albanian. How long had it been since she'd done that? She thought in Albanian only when speaking to Mama and Baba. Never in school. She smiled grimly, then—carefully, methodically—dried herself and put on her street clothes. Next she gathered up her practice uniform, her freshly laundered game uniform, her shin guards, and her mouth guard and took them all through the swinging door to the coach's office. She carefully folded her practice uniform into a square and laid everything down on the desk in a neat stack. With a sheet of paper torn from her notebook she scribbled a short note for Mrs. Rogers and laid it on top of the pile.

Then she walked out the school door into the crisp autumn air. Mehmet was waiting for her, as he used to back in Kosovo. She could see that someone had bloodied his nose. He had tried to wash it away, but there were still traces of blood around his nostrils. She did not have the strength to ask him why. They walked home in silence.

Mama and Baba were both home. There was no work for them that day. "What happened?" Mama asked, looking back and forth from Meli's face to Mehmet's.

"I'm going home," Mehmet said.

Baba turned off the TV and got up. "What is going on?"

"I am going home," Mehmet said again. "I hate America."

128

Baba put his arm around Mehmet's shoulder. "You must tell me what happened, Mehmet."

Mehmet looked at the floor. "They were all swearing against the terrorists. Then they said all Muslims are terrorists, and Americans must kill them all before they destroy America. And then . . ." Meli could see how close to tears he was in his anger. "And then I said, 'I am Muslim. Will you kill me?' So"—he blew out his breath—"so they tried." He wiped his nose on the back of his hand, making it bleed again. "I am never going back to that school. They think I am like those terrorists. They hate me." He looked up defiantly into Baba's face. "Well, I hate them. We are even."

"And you, Meli?" Mama asked quietly.

She didn't want to cry. Somehow, if she did, Brittany would win. "I quit the team," she said.

"What?" Baba had turned from Mehmet and was now looking at her. "What did you say, Meli?"

"I quit."

"Oh, no," Baba said. "No quitting. You must go back. Both of you must go back to school. Go back to the team." He took his handkerchief from his pocket and carefully wiped the blood from Mehmet's face. "Don't you see, son? If you don't go back, the terrorists will win. You can't let them win. You have to go back."

"Never," said Mehmet. He tossed his head and broke free from Baba's grip, as though he were a wild animal intent on escaping a trap. "Never. I am going home."

"This is your home," Baba said.

Mehmet glared at him, his eyes flashing.

"Your home is here with your family." Baba's voice was quiet but strong like steel.

Meli held her breath. It was as though she were watching a duel. If Baba lost . . .

It was Mehmet who dropped his gaze, turned on his heel, and went to the boys' bedroom. The door didn't quite slam behind him. Meli let out a long breath. Baba and Mama looked at each other; then without a word, Baba went back and sank into his chair.

"Come, Meli," Mama said. "Let's make your baba some coffee."

SIXTEEN

Country of the Heart

MEHMET DIDN'T COME OUT OF HIS ROOM FOR DINNER. The rest of them ate in silence, glancing every now and then in the direction of his closed door. "Shall I?" Mama said once.

Baba shook his head.

Meli wanted to go to her brother. Didn't she herself know what he had gone through that day at school? The stares. The whispers. No one had beaten her physically, but they had done enough. Hadn't that scene in the locker room hurt as much as punches to her body? She thought of Rachel, shamefaced but doing what Brittany ordered her to. Zana would never have betrayed her. Friends didn't do that. The bite Meli was trying to swallow lodged in her throat.

"I'm not hungry," she said finally. "I think I'll go—"

"No, Meli," Baba said quietly. "Don't leave us. We have to hold on to each other."

Suddenly, she was back in Kosovo during those terrible times. Yes, they must hold on to each other. War, like a tiger prowling in the shadows, had followed their scent, and now it had them in its sight and was ready to pounce. Their only protection was to stay together. Mehmet had to understand that. How could she make him understand?

She knew he couldn't carry out his threat to return to

131

Kosovo. Even at sixteen he was still a boy. He didn't have money for airfare, or any idea of how to get the proper papers. But his fury frightened her all the same. He had been so much better lately; sometimes he was nearly the old Mehmet, the one she had known before the day he'd disappeared, the day of the pelican. Now it felt as though she had lost her brother all over again. *Don't you see, Mehmet? It's like Baba always said. We have to hold on to each other!*

Did those bullies know the damage they had done to someone who was just beginning to heal? Did they care? It was bad enough to feel alone, as Meli did, deserted by the only person she had dared to think of as a friend, but to have such hatred? And yet, and yet, she herself had tasted that corrosive poison. That very afternoon, looking into Brittany's face, she had seen the hated Serbs. Baba was right. Hate made no sense. They must not let it eat away at their souls. They would become like the very ones they hated. She wanted to bang on Mehmet's door and scream at him, *Don't let them do this to you! Don't do it to yourself!* But she just sat there, staring at her plate.

After she and Mama had washed the dishes, she went to her room and tried to do her homework. Baba had said they must go back to school. But how could she unless Mehmet went as well? Even though she rarely saw him at school, she had to know that he was there—that they were holding together against those who despised them.

She dimly heard the telephone ring in the kitchen and didn't think to wonder who might be calling. But before long Baba knocked on her half-open door. "Meli, are you dressed?"

"Yes, Baba." She whispered so as not to wake Vlora, who was sleeping peacefully in the other bed.

"Wash your face and comb your hair. We have visitors coming."

Visitors? At nine o'clock at night?

Then she heard Baba at Mehmet's door. She didn't want to listen to them argue. She couldn't bear it. She went quickly to the bathroom and washed her face. She patted down her hair and then went into the kitchen, where Mama was busy making coffee. She had changed into her nicest dress.

"Mama?"

"Take some chairs from the kitchen into the parlor, Meli. We need more chairs in there."

As she was bringing in a second chair, Baba and Mehmet emerged from the boys' room. "Help your sister, Mehmet," Baba said.

Mehmet brought in a chair and sat down on it, his body as stiff as a pole. Meli and Mama sat on the others. She waited for some explanation from Baba, but none came. At length they could hear footsteps on the stairs. It sounded like a number of people. *Police! They are going to arrest us for being Muslim.* No, that was crazy. Police didn't call ahead to say they were coming. And Mama wouldn't be dressed up and making coffee if she thought they were all going to be hauled off to jail. It was a ridiculous fear. Still, it was a few seconds before her heart stopped racing. Just some of the welcomers, surely. But why would they come so late at night?

At the knock, Baba nodded at Meli, so she got up and opened the door. The first person she saw in the dark hallway was Mrs. Rogers; just behind her was Mr. Marcello, and with him Adona. Why was Adona here? They hadn't needed a translator for months. Mehmet or she or one of the other children had done all

133

the translating for their parents. The three visitors were in the process of taking off their shoes. Adona must have told the others to. Americans didn't seem to know how important it was.

"Let the guests in, Meli," Baba said. He and Mama stood up.

When Mehmet saw his coach, he started for his bedroom, but Baba grabbed his arm.

"How are you, Meli?" Mrs. Rogers asked.

Meli tried to smile back, but her face felt frozen.

Adona stepped forward and said to Baba in Albanian, "These are the children's coaches for playing soccer." She introduced Mrs. Rogers and Mr. Marcello to Mama and Baba. The adults shook hands formally. Then Baba indicated that everyone, including Mehmet, was to take a seat. The three guests sat down on the couch.

"I have made coffee," Mama said shyly to Adona. "Shall I bring it out? We don't have any cola or mineral water, but . . ."

Adona shook her head. "I don't think so," she said. "It's late. They won't stay long."

Mr. Marcello was sitting on the edge of the couch cushion. He had taken off his baseball cap and was playing with it. The light from the ceiling fixture seemed to bounce off his bald scalp. Finally, without looking at Baba, he spoke to Adona.

"Tell Mr. Lleshi," the coach said, "that I've come to apologize for what happened to his son today."

Adona translated. Mehmet sat like a stone on the kitchen chair, his lips tight, a bruise on his face dark against his red cheek. Meli could still see the dried blood in his nostrils.

"Tell him," the coach continued, "that it will never happen again. I will not tolerate this kind of behavior. Tomorrow those boys are off the team. For good." As Adona translated, Meli saw that Mr. Marcello had a hole in one of his socks. She could see his big toe sticking out like a tiny bald head. *Poor man,* she thought. *How hard this must be for him.* She glanced at Mehmet to see if he felt any pity for his coach. If he did, there was no sign of it.

"And you should tell Mr. and Mrs. Lleshi that I totally agree with Coach Marcello," Mrs. Rogers said. "I am cutting every girl who took part in that scene in the locker room today."

But that would be the whole team! Meli thought, and then wondered how her coach had found out what had happened. Someone must have been ashamed and told her. Meli hoped it had been Rachel.

"I should have been there. I'm usually just next door in my office, but I had been called to the main office, so I wasn't there when it happened. Otherwise . . . I cannot tell you how sorry I am."

Baba listened, his head bent toward the translator to make sure he understood every word. When Adona finished, he looked up at the coaches. "Sank you," he said. Then he turned back to Adona. "Tell the kind teachers that it would not be a good thing to remove those boys and girls from their teams. They will only become bitter and hate my children all the more. Tell the teachers that my children are strong. They have endured many hard things in their short lives. They can also endure this." He waited for Adona to say the words in English; when she paused, he continued. "Tell them my children wish to be respected as fellow teammates and not despised because of their heritage. That is the way of the old country. This is America, tell them. In America, everyone has a new beginning."

When Adona finished translating, Mrs. Rogers smiled, first at Baba and then at Meli. "And what about you, Meli?"

she asked softly. "Do you agree? Should I let everyone stay on the team?"

"Yes, like Baba said."

"Even Brittany?"

"You can't have a team without a goalkeeper."

Coach Marcello turned and spoke directly to Mehmet. "What about you, Mehmet? How do you feel about this?"

Mehmet didn't answer. He sat very still, his eyes on the floor.

"Tell the teacher," Baba said, speaking to Adona but looking all the while at Mehmet, "tell the teacher that my son has endured much more painful hardship than this. As a child, he was once in a Serbian jail, where he was beaten and left in a field to die." As Adona translated, Meli saw Mr. Marcello's eyes widen. Mrs. Rogers gasped. "He is very brave, my son," Baba continued, "and I am very proud of him. He will do the right thing. You will see."

Now Mehmet looked up at Baba, and for a moment Meli imagined she saw tears in her brother's eyes. He did not wait for Adona to finish her translation before he said quietly, "Baba is right. One man does not make a team. We must play together, or there is no game."

Coach Marcello's hands stopped fiddling with his cap. He cleared his throat. "Thank you, Mehmet," he said. Then, very quietly, so that Meli did not hear it until it was repeated in her own language: "He says to tell you, Mr. Lleshi, that you are a good man, and he hopes that he will be as good a father to his children as you are to yours."

"Tell the kind teachers," Baba answered, "that Mehmet and Meli will be back for practice tomorrow."

❈ ❈ ❈

136

The next morning Meli found Rachel waiting at her locker. "Don't hate me," she blurted out. "I was scared. That's no excuse, I know, but—"

"You told Mrs. Rogers, didn't you?"

"Yes, but . . ."

"That was brave, Rachel."

"I should never have let Brittany bully me. I hate myself, so I know you must hate me."

She looked so miserable that Meli reached out and touched her arm. "I could never hate you, Rachel. You're the one person who has always been kind to me."

"Until yesterday. Yesterday . . ."

"My baba says hate makes no sense. He's right. I want to forget about yesterday, okay?"

"Really?"

"Really."

It would be a long time before she and Rachel would eat a sack of salt together, but this was a beginning, wasn't it?

❊ ❊ ❊

Although it wasn't the end of stares in the hallways and whispers in the cafeteria, things were different at school after that. Perhaps it was because Mehmet was different. He was still the best player, but now he was less arrogant, more sharing. Even the boys who had attacked him were forced to respect him.

Meli still worried about her brother. She wanted the last trace of his bitterness to dissolve. She wanted him to slap the other boys on their backsides and tell stupid jokes, which, knowing Mehmet, was most unlikely to happen. But he was trying to make Baba proud of him; that was clear. On Sunday afternoons he began to coach a soccer team for Isuf and Adil and their many little friends, and when Mehmet talked with the younger boys, she could see something of Baba's gentleness growing in him. Every now and then he spoke of returning home, but only when Kosovo was recognized as a nation, not so long as NATO insisted it was still simply a region of Serbia. "Only when we are a free country," he said.

One day, to her own surprise, she realized that she was no longer thinking of going back home to Kosovo. Not because she thought America was a perfect country. If it were a perfect country, Baba would have a good job by now, and Mama wouldn't have to clean motel rooms. Being Muslim or Christian or Jewish or nothing at all wouldn't matter, and the president wouldn't be talking about going to war in yet another Muslim land. Perhaps, though, there were no perfect countries. America was their new beginning, as Baba said, and she was beginning to like the person she was becoming. She had a real friend now. Rachel was not Zana, but she was Rachel, and Meli liked and trusted her.

Of course, some days she thought of Kosovo and felt a wave of homesickness for the things and people she had loved there. She longed for Granny and her funny old ways. She wished she could put flowers on Granny's grave and have coffee with Uncle Fadil and Auntie Burbuqe and Nexima. The twins were talking now. She wanted to talk to them before she forgot all her Albanian, which she knew was getting all mixed up with English words and no longer pure.

She wished she could know where Zana was. Meli had written more letters. None had been answered. She had asked Uncle Fadil, but the new family living in Zana's house had no idea what had happened to the previous owners. Meli dreamed one night that she was walking along the street in a strange American city, and coming toward her on the sidewalk was Zana, looking just as she had the last time Meli had seen her, when they were both eleven years old and misbehaving in Mr. Uka's school. She felt homesick all the next day.

But the homesickness passed. The family had held together. America was home now.

HISTORICAL NOTE

The history of Kosovo is a long and tangled one, and, as in all historical accounts, everything depends on who is telling the story. Kosovars like to recall their great hero Gjergi Kastrioti, better known as Skanderbeg. Skanderbeg was a fifteenth-century prince who fought the invasion of the Ottoman Turks. After his death, the Ottomans prevailed and completely occupied Albanian lands for 425 years. In the late nineteenth and early twentieth centuries, when "Turkey in Europe," as the Balkan portion of the Ottoman Empire was sometimes known, began to break up, there was no way to go back to the national boundaries of pre-Ottoman days. Much of the territory had become part of the Austro-Hungarian Empire. After the empire was defeated in World War I, the Kingdom of the Serbs, Croats, and Slovenes was formed from the southern Slav territories. Its name was changed in 1929 to the Kingdom of Yugoslavia, which literally means "South Slav," and the Federal People's Republic of Yugoslavia was formed after World War II under the former freedom fighter known as Marshall Tito. In 1963 the country was once again renamed, this time as the Socialist Federal Republic of Yugoslavia, or SFRY, and it was made up of six Socialist Republics, SR Bosnia and Herzegovina, SR Croatia, SR Macedonia, SR Montenegro, SR Slovenia, and SR Serbia, which included the autonomous provinces of Vojvodina, Kosovo, and Metohija (later included as part of Kosovo). Although there were Serbs and other minorities living in Kosovo, under Tito Kosovo's leaders were, by and large, Albanian Kosovars, as they made up the majority of the population.

When Tito died in 1980, there was a struggle for the control in Yugoslavia. In the Republic of Serbia, Slobodan Milosević began to take power, and in 1989 he was able to change the constitution in such a way as to reduce the autonomy of Kosovo and put Serbs in charge. Many Albanians lost their jobs and found their activities restricted.

In 1990 Albanian Kosovars proclaimed the Republic of Kosovo, and in unsanctioned elections chose as president a literary scholar and pacifist, Ibrahim Rugova, who created a shadow government that had no actual power. When Bosnia proclaimed its independence from the Federal Republic of Yugoslavia (FRY) in 1991, a bloody war ensued, in which the better-armed Bosnian Serbs carried out a policy of "ethnic cleansing" designed to eliminate the Muslim population of Bosnia. NATO intervened on behalf of the Bosnian Muslims and brokered a settlement. Eventually, Europe and the United States recognized Bosnia—as well as Slovenia and Croatia, whose declarations of independence had preceded Bosnia's—as an independent nation, but not Kosovo, which was to remain a province of FRY, which by 1992 consisted only of Serbia and Montenegro.

In the early nineties, the Kosovo Liberation Army (KLA) grew out of small groups of nationalistic guerrillas making occasional attacks against Serbian authorities in Kosovo. The Serbs reacted by further acts of repression against Albanian citizens, exemplified by the massacre of the Jashari family in March 1998.

Although the U.S. secretary of state Madeleine Albright declared on March 7, "We are not going to stand by and watch the Serbian authorities do in Kosovo what they can no longer get away with doing in Bosnia," American and European governments did little more than talk and threaten while Serbian atrocities continued. There were counterattacks from the growing KLA resistance, and those were met with more violence from the Serbian police as well as soldiers from Milosević's FRY army. Attempts to negotiate a settlement with President Milosević failed repeatedly, and a NATO bombing campaign, hitting targets in both Kosovo and Serbia proper, commenced in March 1999. FRY military and Serb paramilitary troops then began an attempt to clear Kosovo of all its Albanian citizens, who up until then had made up about 90 percent of the population. During this terrible process of so-called ethnic cleansing, many Albanians were massacred and many Albanian women were raped. Homes and farms were routinely looted and then burned to prevent their Albanian owners from ever returning.

In June 1999 NATO reached an agreement with FRY regarding a withdrawal of Serbian troops from Kosovo, and Albanian Kosovars began to return from the refugee camps to which they had fled or been driven. Tragically, there were many acts of revenge committed against the remaining Serb population, causing a northward flight of Serbs from Kosovo to Serbia. President Milosević was indicted for war crimes in 1999 but was not brought to trial until 2002; he died in prison in 2006 before a verdict was reached.

As part of the June 1999 settlement, a NATO force known as KFOR entered Kosovo to preserve order and provide aid in the devastated country; as of spring 2009 it still maintained a presence in Kosovo. On February 17, 2008, the Assembly of Kosovo's Provisional Institutions of Self-Government declared the Republic of Kosova an independent nation. The Albanian Kosovar double-headed eagle flag was disallowed by the UN, so Kosova's current flag shows a map of the country with six stars—each star representing one of Kosova's major ethnic groups. This is significant, for the new constitution promises to protect the rights of minorities (including Serbs) and provide guaranteed ethnic representation in the government. The Republic of Kosova—or as the UN still calls it, Kosovo—has been recognized by more than forty nations, including the United States, but, at this writing, more than twenty nations, including Serbia and Russia, still refuse recognition.

The Lleshis' story ends in America, but the story of their native land is still being written. We can only hope that those who have survived so much terror and devastation will be able to build a strong and peaceful nation.

ACKNOWLEDGMENTS

This book came out of my acquaintance with the Haxhiu family, who came to Vermont in 1999 under the sponsorship of the First Presbyterian Church of Barre. Among the many actual "welcomers" who did much to help the Haxhius feel at home in this country our pastors, Carl and Gina Hilton–Van Osdall, and Steve and Wendy Dale, deserve particular mention. It was Steve who gave me the idea to write about one Kosovar family's experience, which I did initially in a newspaper breakfast serial titled *Long Road Home*. The person who has made the writing of this book possible is Mark Orfila, who lived for a number of years in Kosovo, both before and after the terrible events of 1998–99. He and his wife also worked in a Macedonian refugee camp. I cannot thank Mark enough for all his help. And, finally, I must once again thank my chief supporters: my editor, Virginia Buckley, and my husband, John Paterson.